REMNANTS

Nikki Salmon

Published 2019

ISBN/SKU: 9780578514383
ISBN Complete: 978-0-578-51438-3

PRINTED IN THE UNITED STATES OF AMERICA

To those who have lost a mortal
but gained an angel.

PROLOGUE

'Winter charged in like the bull upon the matador.

She was clothed in dark attire – her cloak, the darkest of grey with thickness to shield her from the light of the sun.

In her hand she bore a large piece of solidified water. The tip was sharp and spiked.

Then....in one quick swipe; she silenced autumn.

She was cold!

After all, she had a reputation to uphold.

Winter froze hearts and painted many things blue.

She wasn't likeable. In her eyes everyone loved summer.

But summer needed to rejuvenate. She needs her beautiful rest.

And though the two had never met. What she knew for sure was that summer was loud and obnoxious. And most of all she was filth.

So, she vowed to rid the Earth of her musty stench.

Autumn, she knew, and she was much too weak and... Spring whom she had met, was far too kind. Always prancing around like some giddy headed child.

Winter sent rain and she made it pour and then she dusted the land with snow.

From morning until night... It snowed.

Then morning came.'

"Bird!" Quilt yelled from upstairs. His voice filled with a sense of urgency.

This was the second time he had interrupted her since she started reading. She quickly placed the leather holder between the pages and closed the book.

CONTENTS

CHAPTER ONE

Anniversary

"You two were so adorable" Camille said as she watched the home video being played. The teenagers on the screen chased each other around the bank of the pool despite the eyes of the adults glowering towards them.

"We still are," Dove replied as she gently placed a kiss on Quilt's lips. He smiled, the woman he loved had been overjoyed with his surprise gathering of family and friends to celebrate their three years of marriage. He was far more than pleased watching her smile. "Okay, pause it," she yelled with excitement. "Right there!" She pointed at the screen. "That's the moment I knew." She snuggled closer in his arms as they all watched as a fourteen-year-old boy wiped away the traces of blood from her knee from a fall she had obtained moments before. "That's when I knew the boy next door was the one."

Young Quilt was always caring when it came to Dove.

He grinned widely. He had known the woman for a lifetime and yet she still possessed the ability to make him feel like every day was new. It was something to see a grown man blush.

"Okay, that's enough affection. Let's go eat, after all I didn't spend half the day cooking for our guest not to enjoy the food." Dove's mother retrieved the remote from the round wooden table and quickly paused the home movie. Mrs. Williams was tall and slender built. Her middle child had bared much of the same traits has her mother.

"I thought the food was catered." Quilt smiled devilishly. He was very much a part of planning every detail.

"You always did have an honest trait," Mrs. Williams said. "But perhaps, in this instance you could allow me to take some credit since you wouldn't allow me to cook." She smiled back at him. Quilt had been a stellar son in law and although she was a bit of a control freak, she did allow him to have complete control of planning the surprise party.

"Love you, Mom," he told her as he pulled her in for a hug and a kiss on her cheek. Just then his own mother interrupted.

"Darling, be a good boy and grab you mother a glass of champagne, will you?" The ex-Mrs. Matthew requested.

"Yes mother," he replied, also placing a kiss on her cheek before walking away to fulfill her order.

"Dana, when will these two decide to give us grand babies? For goodness sake, it's been three years of marriage. Lord knows I'm not getting any younger."

"Dove promised me that they would be trying very soon. Fingers crossed."

"What are you two smiling about?" Dove questioned as she walked towards to her mother. She hugged her mother's shoulder, brushing back strands of hair from her face.

Neither of the elder ladies responded with words but their smiles were mischievous.

Quilt made his way over with two glasses of sparkling champagne. He passed one to his mom and offered the other to Dove as his mother in law took a sip of the glass of wine in her hand.

"Honey," she said disapprovingly, "Now you know I shouldn't be drinking."

The two older ladies gasped with excitement.

Dove never mentioned it to anyone, but for two years the couple had tried to conceive. There had been a few times she thought she had been successful but each time she would only be left with disappointment. It had been quite a difficult journey. One that had only left her feeling inadequate and ashamed... as if she was less of a woman if she couldn't bear a child. The indignity of being infertile had kept her from sharing any information with anyone, even from her sisters.

"Slow down medaling moms. I'm on antibiotics for a sinus infection. Two more days and I'll be able to drink all the champagne I want." Dove smiled at them. Then she softly placed a kiss on her husband lips.

"Some birds are meant to be caged," Quilt whispered

"Happy anniversary sweetheart," Dove whispered between slightly parted lips.

Dove closed her eyes for a moment. She wanted to take everything in. The gratitude she felt. The unbelievable feeling of being the luckiest girl in the world.

How often does a teenage girl fall in love with a teenage boy and end up marrying the love of her life? After her father died when she was nineteen, Quilt had pretty much become the only male presence in her life. Even after years had passed, her mother had decided there would never be anyone good enough to replace her dad. She found comfort in solitude.

"How are you holding up?" Quilt asked as he searched her face for answers. "How's the pain?"

"It's okay," she replied

"You're lying." He half smiled. "I can tell you're hurting." He possessed the uncanny ability to decipher her expressions.

"Okay, maybe it hurts a little," she smiled.

"You're still lying." And this time a laugh escaped him as he saw her frustrated expression for not being able to conceal her pain. "I will thank our guess for coming, run you a nice hot bath and I will have a nice serving of Amoxicillin and Percocet when you get out."

He took her hand and they walked towards the entertainment room.

Majority of the guests stood socializing. They were all in such good spirits that she hated Quilt had decided it would end.

"....and it is a miracle drug. I've successfully treated a patient suffering from post-traumatic-stress by suppressing her negative memories that were linked to pain receptors." Mrs. Williams bragged to one of the guests who shared the same passion for medicine. She continued to elaborate but was soon interrupted by Robyn.

"Mom can you join my conversation for a brief minute?" She asked.

"Oh, Dove!" She exclaimed. Upon seeing her sister enter the room. Robyn pulled her arm towards the center of the room.

Dove still held on to Quilt's hand, also pulling him with her.

"Remember that summer you snuck out of the house and went to the movies with some of your friends, and you guys ended up getting arrested?"

"Yes, I remember it very well," she smiled. "Mom bailed us out... dad was just out from the hospital and she made us promise not to say a word about it."

"Yes exactly!" She exclaimed. "Now can you tell my husband here, that Raven was the one that told dad." Robyn said, folding her arms with an air of confidence.

"As I recall, it was you Robyn." She forced a smile as she tried to suppress a sharp pain that had done a somersault across her stomach. "You were the one that told dad. I overheard the entire conversation as you ratted me out. I had to spend an entire summer indoors."

Raven covered her wide-open mouth as she squealed with pleasure. "See Dennis, your wife is not that innocent. She's a rat."

They all laughed as Robyn playfully hung her head in defeat.

Another jolt of pain forced Dove to grimace. Though she was able to suppress it before, this time it was quite visible, yet it went undetected by the eyes in the room, except from Quilt.

"Everyone, can I have your attention please," he yelled. "First, Dove and I would sincerely like to thank each one of you for coming out tonight and celebrating this special day with us. But unfortunately, this wonderful night has to come to an end."

The crowd expressed their displeasure, although it was in a very playful way.

"We have a very long day tomorrow and..."

"...and I'm sure a very long night as well," Raven interrupted, adding a wink.

"Oh Raye, why do you always have to be a little extra. Get your coat," Mrs. Williams ordered. "Dove," she continued. "You look tired honey, make sure you get some rest tonight."

She hugged her daughter and placed a kiss on her cheek and she continued to Quilt, "I love you son, take care of my girl."

The couple said their goodbyes to all the guests before retreating to their bedroom.

Quilt ran a nice warm bath for his wife. He eyed her small frame as his face covered with concerned upon meeting her sunken eyes. Without the make-up, they were just so much more noticeable. He took his wife's hands before carefully placing her into the bath, lowering her gently as if she was a porcelain doll that would break at the slightest touch.

"Thanks babe." She smiled weakly then sunk her body until it was fully submerged in the water, only allowing her head to rest against the hard enamel tub.

He squeezed her hand twice before making his way out.

The sacrifices Quilt had made to keep his wife happy only demonstrated unmistakably and irrevocably the power she possessed over him. He was against the risky procedure, had ensured her that he would be fine if they never had kids, but his wife was stubborn, and he knew her heart's every desire. She wanted to be a mother and he just couldn't take that away from her. But seeing her in so much pain and watching her suffer from complications from the procedure had made him question whether he should've said no. After all, they were a team and they had long since decided that one would never make an important decision without being in complete agreement with the other.

"Did you take your pain pill?" He asked.

She nodded.

"What about the other?"

"Yes," she nodded again.

He climbed into bed and cuddled up next to her, his arms providing comfort and security as they drifted into a time of darkness and silence.

CHAPTER TWO

This Is Us

The night passed. Dove woke up to the sound of rustling leaves and wind howling. Autumn had said its goodbye yesterday. She knew it had to be very cold out and sighed happily that she had taken the full two months off work. She had enjoyed being the social butterfly, but in the last few days she had come to really appreciate the time away from teaching and spending quiet time with Quilt. He had also taken a few days off from the office though he would still attempt to work on designs at home.

Reluctantly, she crawled from between the blue cotton sheets and made her way towards the smell of fresh blueberries.

Quilt stood by the gas stove, a spatula in one hand, the other held the handle of the cast iron skillet, his hand briskly stirring the eggs. Dove leaned against the white wooden panel, her arms crossed over her chest. She smiled as she admired her husband as he awkwardly twisted the utensil. Quilt had never cooked a day in his life but there he stood, bending over a hot stove making scrambled eggs while batter dribbled down the side of the waffle maker. The kitchen was a mess and although she was slightly obsessive when it came to her kitchen, she really didn't mind that there were egg shells scattered across the counter and drops of milk spilled on the floor. He scooped an adequate amount of eggs on a plate, and on the side he added a mixture of fresh strawberries, blueberries and her favorite, concord grapes. He poured her tea in the cup with the words 'The Mrs.', and poured his own in the matching 'The Mr.' cup, which he slightly overfilled, causing the substance to spill over. Dove placed her fingers over her lips as she tried to hold back the giggles at seeing how he was struggling, but how adorable he looked trying to keep it together.

Quilt turned at sensing her presence.

"What are you doing?" he asked. "It's called breakfast in bed, not out of bed." He said with a frown.

She walked over to the kitchen table and pulled out a chair, the one facing the window that offered the street view. "Quilt, please," she begged. "I am so sick of being in bed. Can we just sit here and eat breakfast?"

His silence made her a little nervous.

"It's such a nice day out, maybe we could even sit on the patio?" She smiled. She knew she was pushing it. Her doctor had given her very strict orders to rest for a few weeks and Quilt was never one to go half on anything. He would see everything through to the end. That's one reason he became such a successful architect. She would undoubtedly be fully rested as the doctor ordered, but now on day number six, she started feeling like it had been forever since she last felt the crisp air on her face. The New England foliage was the most glorious to view at this time of the year. She could see the trees across the street with their kaleidoscope of colors and as the wind blew, she watched as each leave descended onto the ground.

"Okay, we'll eat breakfast here." He laid the plates with scrambled eggs and fruits, gently kissed her lips and made his way back to grab the two cups of vanilla chai.

"Talk to me," he said as he sat down next to her. "I hate to see you sad and right now you are giving me puppy eyes, you know I can't resist your puppy eyes."

The corner of her mouth quirked up to replace her pouted lips.

"Talk to me babe," he said. Quilt reached for her hand and placed it against his lips.

"I've been thinking about a lot of what if's... like what if this procedure doesn't work? There's always the possibility that my endometriosis will return... and-"

"But what if it doesn't," he reassured her. And at that very moment a light trickled through the window casting an indigo color in the room. A hint of the light came across his face and all doubts in her head began to erase, as in that moment, she remembered who her husband was... the man who always made the impossible happen.

He comforted her some more and placed his arms around her, giving her the warmest embrace. "I love you my darling and if it will make you happy then yes, we can go sit on the porch swing and relax, much like we'll do when we're old and grey with our children."

"Old and grey with grandbabies," she smiled with pleasure. Nothing else excited her more than that thought.

They sat cuddling on the straight back swing made of dried red shorea. It was finely crafted and built to withstand the New England weather. She found peace in the day.

The day was cooler, bringing about a wave of fresh air that felt soothing to the soul. The kind of day that made you want to only sip on warm soup and hot cocoa.

It was the kind of day that jack o lanterns perched on porches, squirrels rustled in the leaves to find nuts, and mouths watered from the smell of the neighbors baking pumpkin pies. The kind of day where two cozied up and reminisced about the lost days of summer.

"Remember the day when we graduated high school and our parents officially allowed us to stay out until midnight for the first time?"

Quilt smiled as the memories came flooding back. "How could I forget? It was the night we went to Shane 'Skyscraper' Cooper's house party and we made the very bad decision to drink from the punch bowl."

"Best punch I've ever tasted," Dove laughed.

"We both got unbelievably drunk and you had the brilliant idea of filling balloons up with water and throwing them from the rooftop. I completely went along with the idea because that what the most beautiful girl in school wanted." He looked at her with admiration. Quilt reached for her head and pulled it closer so that he could gently stroke her hair.

They say a man is not supposed to cry, but every time he thought about the pain she has suffered from last year's miscarriage, he couldn't help it. He would never let her see the tears in his eyes because he had to be strong... for himself, but mostly for her. He quickly pushed the sad memories back and snapped back to the happy one. "I remembered you mistakenly dropping a water balloon on Skyscraper's head and he went ballistic. Remember how we both tried to run by climbing down the drain pipe?" Her laughter filled the air.

"Yes, and I ended up falling."

"Thank God for that bush or that fracture would've been a lot worse," she added.

"Second best fall I've ever taken." Quilt smiled. "...and the day I fell for you was the first."

"How did I get so lucky?" she asked.

It's not luck, Dove, Quilt answered in his head. "It was destiny."

"Promise me whatever storms may come... we will conquer them together. Just don't ever leave me."

"Never my love. Never!"

A moment passed before she erupted in a burst of laughter.

"What's so funny?" He asked.

"I was thinking about Skyscraper and if he had caught us that night. He had such a gigantic physique so I'm sure we both would've ended up with a broken leg anyways. So, in a way I kind of saved you."

"My hero," he teased.

"I love you darling."

"I love you more," he replied.

It was a little after six when they decided to make their way back into the house, but not before taking one long glance at the sun as it set in the sky.

CHAPTER THREE

Goons and Goblins

The day felt much colder than the sixty-two degrees weather that had been predicted. It felt as if the temperature had somehow dipped into the low forties. Dove parked her car in the driveway and retrieved the two brown bags of groceries from the trunk. She struggled a bit with the heavy load of milk, eggs and candy... tons of candy. She smiled to herself as the thought of the many recipes she had plan to create for the Halloween party that night. Just then a black cat crossed her path, almost brushing against her feet. It startled her and for a second, she panicked, dropping one of the bags.

"Shit!" she shouted. She heard the eggs cracking in the bag.

This had been a very strange day but then again, the entirety of 2016 had presented many challenges. On top of everything, it was Monday and Halloween, so she was aware it wouldn't be an easy day.

She grabbed the bag from the ground and made her way into the house where she assessed the contents. It appeared that the eggs were the only thing that had suffered any damages. She would just have to ask Raven to pick her some more eggs. Raven was very flexible since she only worked part time as a paralegal. Luckily, today was one of her days off.

The house felt empty but that was okay because tonight it would be filled with the wonderful sounds of kids and grownups. It had been one week since she had been back at work. Quilt had gone back to working in the office. The old house felt empty whenever he worked late nights. The couple had bought it soon after they got married. They both planned on building their dream home but there was just something about this house that had connected with both of them. Maybe it was the wrap around porch, or it could've been the innocuous feature of the front door. Whatever it was, the Victorian house was perfect for them. The only things missing were children and a dog, but she had faith and prayer that these things would come. After all, they had bought a house with four bedrooms. It certainly would be a huge disappointment if they still were not able to fill the empty rooms, even after suffering through such a painful surgery.

In the kitchen sink laid the evidence that Quilt had been up working late. Two Belgian beer glasses, two plates with remnants of the lasagna she had made for dinner, and dessert plates with stains of chocolate frosting. *How did those two get anything done if they were eating like this?* Dove thought for a second. Quilt and stayed up late with his colleague Edmond. She wasn't sure what project they were working on, all she knew was it was a very big deal.

She adjusted the temperature of the water before applying dish detergent to the sponge. She still preferred the old-fashioned way of cleaning dishes, thus the dishwasher only got attention when her work and home was overwhelming. The work of a second-grade teacher was far more hectic than first perceived. Preparing lessons, grading homework or even the endless conferences turned out to be somewhat of a stress.

The water was warm and soothing against her skin. She watched through the kitchen window as the sun's ray of lights got dimmer. For a minute, she thought she saw a reflection of a person inside the house. Her heart began to race, and she immediately turned off the running water. Maybe her mind was playing a trick on her. It had been a long day and she still felt a bit weak. Yet, she knew better than to second guess herself. She looked up again in the glass window, keeping her eyes focused while she reached for the carving knife. Slowly she turned around and walked towards the door.

"Quilt?" She yelled, but there was no response.

She paused, thinking about the fact that she was doing everything similar to every actor on screen in a scary movie, she would usually be shouting at them what not to do.

Dove took a step back into the kitchen and reached for her cellphone that she had left inside of her purse on the kitchen table.

Just when she was about to dial, a slender frame wearing a mask suddenly appeared in the doorway. Her fingers gripped the knife tighter and she could feel the pulsation in her neck. Her arms trembled as she slowly raised the knife...stopping before deciding to lunge. She had recognized the pixie haircut, and the small frame wearing the anorak jacket, with a hood trimmed with faux fur.

"Raven!" she screamed, and loosened her grip on the knife, allowing it to fall from her hand.

She loved her baby sister but at this moment, however, Dove would love to nothing better than to wrap both hands around her neck. Raven had very much succeeded in bringing her close to pissing herself.

"What in the hell are you doing?" Dove yelled as she took a step towards her sister. "I could've killed you." She screamed some more, and the veins were protruding on her forehead.

"Chill!" Raven replied as she took a few steps back. "It's Halloween. Don't be such a grump." She removed the hockey mask from her face.

"Don't be such as grump?" Dove shouted. "Don't be such as grump," she repeated as if she was still in disbelief that her sister had not processed the tragic events that could've occurred.

Raven took two more steps back.

"You know at twenty-two I really wish you could not be so immature."

"Oh, you wished I was more mature?" She mocked in a childlike voice and she dashed towards the living room as she saw the rigid, cold hard stare that consumed Dove's eyes.

"I am going to kill you," she shouted as she chased her around the living room before pinning her to the floor.

"It's Halloween!" Raven yelled as she desperately tried to free her arms.

They both ignored the sound of the key turning in the door as they both continued grunting at each other. The door to the living room opened and Quilt entered. His head tilted to the side upon seeing the two ladies wrestling on the floor.

"Quilt help!" Raven shouted. "Your wife is bat crazy!"

"Well you should've known that before you tried to scare me," she retorted.

Quilt dropped his briefcase and he hurriedly moved to separate the ladies.

He lifted Dove and extended an arm to Raven as he pulled her up from the floor. He had never seen any of the sisters get physical with each other... well, except for that one time in eighth grade, and that time it was between Dove and Robyn, never Raven. His wife had always been so protective of her baby sister.

"Will someone tell me what's going on?" The creases on Quilt's forehead grew tighter.

Raven straightened her clothes and zipped up her jacket. "Maybe you should ask your wife since you're going to take her side anyways." Her eyes were glossy, and water lingered around her pupils. She threw a set of keys on the couch and walked towards the door. "There's your stupid house key that mom gave me, and your damn eggs are on the dining room table." She grabbed the door handle "...and one other thing, I won't be attending your lame ass Halloween party," she said, slamming the door as she exited.

"So, do you want to tell me what that was about?"

Dove threw herself into his arms. Her heartbeat finally stopped racing inside of her chest.

He embraced her and gently stroked the strands of her unruly hair. He actively listened as she described how terrified she had felt believing it was an intruder, but she was even more terrified of the idea that she could've killed her sister.

"I understand babe. You're safe and nothing will ever hurt you as long as I'm around," he whispered.

She closed her eyes, inhaling the scent of him, every part of his 6'o-foot frame made her feel secure. "I expected dinner when I got home, now it's me and you who are going to be wrestling," he teased.

Quilt moved his arm in a quick motion and picked her and they both landed on the couch. He began to tickle her sides. She laughed hysterically even though she hated to be tickled but loved it at the same time.

Their playtime was interrupted by the doorbell.

"Trick or Treat!" The group of three kids yelled.

"...and who are you supposed to be?" Quilt asked.

The small boy responded proudly "Superman." He had a soft voice with a lisp and his perfect little round angelic face lit up at the sight of the lady approaching with the bag of candy.

"Wow!" Dove exclaimed. "You guys must be the Justice League." She bent forward slightly as she handed each kid a pre-filled bag.

The youngest child looked about three years old. He gave her a nod. "I'm Batman," he whispered shyly.

"Well Batman, it is a pleasure to meet you, and you as well Superman and Wonder Woman."

"What do we say?" The lady reminded them.

"Thank you." They shouted simultaneously before waving goodbye.

She watched as their little hands motioned and she listened as their tiny feet made pitter patter noise across the porch. An emptiness crept up inside of her as it was another constant reminder of what she was missing out on. The difficulty of not being able to conceive was a well-guarded secret, even from her closest friends. So many times, she wanted to tell someone, to tell her sisters, to be open about the struggle, but then so many times she had difficulty describing the pain with words. All she knew was how it felt, and no one could completely understand unless it was also their experience. She thought about how she could possibly describe the pain... it was looking at your best friend's sonogram and crying silent tears. It was the agony of listening to her co-workers talk about their babies' first word being 'mama'. It was logging into social networks and seeing the trending family photos. Most of all, it was tear stained pillows, the feeling of emptiness and years of internalizing the idea that infertility made her feel broken.

Quilt looked at his wife. He knew exactly what she was thinking about. He recognized the sadness in her eyes, the longing. They had spent more than a decade together and at times he felt he knew Dove much better than she knew herself. It hadn't mattered that she had suffered a car accident that almost left her paralyzed, and it damn sure wouldn't matter if she wasn't able to bear him a child. He had known since the age of ten that she was something special. She on the other hand, thought of him as her best friend. Together they would break the glass in Mrs. Parker's second floor window playing baseball, and together they stole some fireworks and almost set his parents' house on fire when it ignited with the debris in the gutter. It was also the incident when a sixteen-year-old Quilt took it upon himself to teach his then fifteen-year-old girlfriend to drive, damaging the car and his parents' garage.

"Hey," he said softly, and he unwrapped the paper from a chocolate peanut butter cup.

"Yes?" She responded.

He gently pulled her chin towards him. "Kiss me," he whispered, and she eagerly obliged. She adored the way he would come home, remove his jacket, loosen the button on his shirt and roll up his sleeves. It's when she found him to be his sexiest.

She started with a small peck on the lips... once... twice and a third time. His lips were sweet as if they had been dipped in sugar. His mouth parted her lips and with her eyes closed, she waited for his lips to enter deeper. Quilt smirked as he inserted a piece of peanut butter cup into her mouth. Dove began to squint as if she was tasting a lemon.

"I am going to kill you," she screamed. "You know how I hate peanut butter."

He started to back away as took a step closer to him. He found it very cute when she would act mad, except for the times when she really was angry. That could be scary at times. Her fiery temper was something he'd learnt about in childhood.

"Quilt Matthew, please step forward to face your punishment." She moved in closer, the peanut butter cup with its melted chocolate resting in the middle of her palm.

"Play nice babe," he smiled "This is my favorite shirt."

She shook her head. "You should've thought about that before you tried to kill me with this disgusting candy bar."

He took a step into the house and she sprinted towards him. His hands meet both her wrists and he held them securely so she couldn't move.

"You don't want to do this," he grinned at her.

"Yes, I do."

Something in the way she pouted her lips prompted a flashback of their first kiss. He was fifteen and that moment still replayed as if it was yesterday.

His lips came crashing down on hers and she melted, much like the chocolate in her hands.

She wrapped her arms around his sides, forgetting all about her playful sweet revenge, and as always, his kiss propelled her to a place under a shaded tree. A place where she always felt safe.

He chuckled under his breath, "looks like you got your revenge... you owe me a shirt Mrs. Matthew."

"I will get you all the shirts you need." And they kissed one more time.

"Eww!"

The sound interrupted their embrace.

A couple more trick or treaters stood in the doorway, peering at them through the exterior glass panel. They both giggled. "I guess there is nothing scarier than seeing two adults kiss."

"How appropriate for Halloween," Quilt laughed.

"Okay, can you handle this one by yourself?" She asked. "I need to finish the food for the party."

He kissed her one more time. "Yes Mrs. Matthew," he replied and made his way towards the anxiously awaiting trick-or-treaters.

CHAPTER FOUR

It's A Party

It wasn't that she was in denial, but she had hoped that Raven would've have somehow realized that her actions had been wrong. She had hoped she would still show up to the party.

Robyn was there though, and she was grateful that her older sister had not seemed to have chosen a side in the argument, choosing only to point out what the other could've done more effectively.

Dove smiled as she greeted her sister, who looked ever so uncomfortable dressed up as gothic goddess.

"If I had known the theme was slutty, I would've dressed more appropriately," she smiled cynically, and she spun Dove around to get a better look at the cat woman suit that looked as if it had been painted on. "Mom must be so proud," she teased.

The two embraced. "Oh Robyn! Just promise me you will allow yourself to enjoy the party," Dove smiled.

"Where's your better half?" She asked. And just then she spotted Quilt making his way through the crowd. His tall frame gliding towards them. He was dressed up as his favorite character - Batman. His wife had to practically beg him to wear it because he thought men in tights were humiliating and silly. Nevertheless, he looked like a real-life action hero.

"I see she has gotten to you too Quilt," Robyn scoffed.

Quilt gave her a hug. "You know how persuasive your sister can be." He smiled revealing perfect pearly whites through the gap in the lower part of the face mask. "Can I get you something to drink Robyn?"

"Yes, I'll take a shot of the strongest liquor you've got," she replied.

He chuckled.

"Yes!" Dove exclaimed in delight. "A drunk Robyn and the party will be a memorable one."

"Oh, stop it," Robyn retorted. "Don't act like I've never had a drink before." She rolled her eyes.

"Well hello there Aunt Dove, don't you look hot... Not so bad yourself Uncle Quilt." The girl giggled.

She was petite and barely stood five feet. Her hair was in a high ponytail and her natural curls laid down to her chin. "Sorry I had to show up in this basic costume, it was the only way mom would allow me to dress. I'm eighteen now, why should I still dress up as Cinderella?" She pouted.

"Well, someone should have explained to this teenager that being eighteen doesn't allow you to call yourself an adult unless you are out in the world supporting yourself. Until then, it is still my rules and dressing up in a sexy maid outfit will not be allowed by your parents," Robyn replied.

"Heaven, please listen to your mom. You'll have enough opportunity in college to dress slutty," Dove added mockingly. She enjoyed ruffling Robyn's composure which was always very cool and collected.

Robyn was almost thirty-seven, but she had always been mature beyond her years. Becoming a mother at nineteen had only made her focused and ambitious. Being the first born, her mother had made her responsible. Robyn tried to be the perfectionist, only to please her parents. It was a trait that allowed her to become one of the top CEOs at her company located in Stamford. Dove couldn't remember a time when Robyn wasn't dressed conservatively. Even as teenagers, her thick, curly hair was almost always pulled back in a bun. She wore cardigan sweaters and her brown rimmed glasses enhanced her full beautiful brown eyes. Robyn hated being call a prude, but she was the prude of the family, much like Dove was the wild child, always rebelling against rules, and Raven was forever the clown who didn't take much seriously.

Quilt made his way back with the drinks.

Heaven extended her arm, pretending to reach for one.

"Don't you even think about it!" Her mother scowled at her.

Dove laughed as she excused herself to attend to her other guests.

In the far corner of the entertainment room stood a dark figure. He was of average height and medium build. His face was partially covered by a half white mask. The other half obscured by the dark shadow. She moved closer to get a better glimpse of him and then he smiled, revealing a crooked central incisor, and instantly she felt the familiarity.

"Anthony?" She asked with a bit of uncertainty.

"Hi little bird." He moved forward revealing his face as he walked towards the light.

She ran towards him, hugging him tightly; A minute for every year she had not seen him.

They had all grew up on the same street until his family moved to Boston midway through tenth grade.

Anthony was the undisputed smart kid of the block and the brains behind the infamous 'Pizza Experiment'. The experiment where they all found a lost credit card and decided to order ten boxes of pizza to old Mr. Winterbourne's address. It was a very skilled plot for a bunch of ten and eleven-year old. Mr. Winterbourne lived alone and walked with a cane. He was always very grateful for help around the house.

Anthony decided that each of them would volunteer some form of service that day. He would sweep the yard and would be the lookout, Quilt and Dove would gain access to the house by offering to clean. Once inside the two would use the phone to order the pizza. Quilt was reluctant but gave in after Dove called him a pussy. Ten-years-old and she was already dictating what made everyone brave. The truth was that Quilt had a good heart, probably the most caring heart amongst the group. He knew it wasn't right taking advantage of an old man, but Dove was always a tough one and he did pretty much everything to please her. Ten boxes of pizza were delivered to the house while the old man slept. The neighborhood kids would soon join them in Mr. Winterbourne's garage to enjoy the boxes. It was Quilt that insisted that one box of pizza should be left for the old man.

No crime goes without consequences, and word got out about the pizza ordeal. The three masterminds would find themselves with severe punishment for an entire summer including apologizing to Miss Jennings for using her card and doing whatever task she requested in order to clear the debt. They had been restricted from any social activities and banned from Mr. Winterbourne's house forever. Trouble always seemed to find them in the summer.

"We have a lot to catch up on," she squealed. "How did you find us? Do you have a wife and kids? Where are you living...?"

He chuckled. "I ran into Quilt downtown and he told me about the party. Boyfriend, no kids, and I'm in Boston now. We bought a house and opened a delightful little coffee shop called *Cups*." They walked towards the dining room.

"So, what's up with you and the hubby?" he continued. "Any babies running around yet?"

It usually stung a little when anyone would ask that question, but this time it didn't bring any kind of pain. There was an inner peace now, it was as if she knew that one day she would become a mother. Her entire thought process had changed. It was less about what ifs and more about when.

"No babies yet, but we will be trying soon," she replied.

"You should really try these Zombie cupcakes. They are really delicious." She shifted the subject.

He politely declined, "I've tried just about everything you have here, and I will send you a bill for my gym membership." He smiled.

"What are you two plotting?" Quilt joined the conversation. "Nothing good ever happens when you two start scheming."

"Excuse me but as I recall it was always the three of us and you were always the mastermind," Anthony replied.

Quilt gave a hearty laugh. "Nice try but as I recall, you were always the diabolic one. I'm surprised you didn't show up tonight dressed as the Joker."

They all erupted with laughter.

"I have to agree with my hubby on this one. Tony, you were the ultimate villain. Frankly I was surprised to see you tonight... I thought you would've been in jail by now."

He laughed. "I see you two are still pretty hilarious." He smiled at them fondly "...but seriously. I am so happy things worked out for the two of you. You were the two best friends a kid could have, and I always knew you were meant for each other."

The couple looked at each other, each feeling undeserving of this gift.

"Enough with the kissing," Anthony interrupted. "Throw some music on, I'm ready to party."

It was close to midnight when the party came to an end. Dove hated to see everyone go, especially since the crowd was clearly enjoying themselves.

She must've looked at the door a hundred times throughout the night with the hope that Raven would walk through, but she never showed.

Music ceased.

People groaned.

Monsters departed into the night.

Two lovers embraced.

Hearts beat against each other until sleep stole the night.

CHAPTER FIVE

Just Two Aiming For Three

The waiter stood about six feet tall. His name was Crimson, and it was a perfect fit for the man with the red hair and tan freckles that covered his face. He smiled revealing yellow stained teeth, perhaps a smoker. His voice was raspy, and his speech was slow as he carefully explained the different entrees for the night.

"....and for the specials we have Lobster, poached in a beurre monte, topped with a buttery cream sauce and served on a bed of sautéed spinach."

"That sounds delicious," said Quilt. "Can we have just a few more minutes with the menu? But in the meantime, we will take a bottle of Cabernet Sauvignon."

"Yes sir," he replied.

The restaurant was extremely packed and appeared to be at capacity.

Winter had begun a very brutal season, especially in New England, prompting the couple to escape to one of their favorite vacation spots in Florida. The get-away had been perfect, especially since Dove was in her ovulation cycle. A romantic trip could only increase her chances of fertilization.

This was St. George, and if perfection existed, then this was it. The serenity of the ocean, white sands and a very private beach house in one of the most secluded areas.

Solo por Dos turned out to be the best restaurant in St. George if romance was the goal. The title alone literally meant "for two". Everything was set up to accommodate pairs. The tables, the decorations on the walls, even the man playing the piano with a partner. He stroked the keys while she sang her best rendition of Misty Blue.

The upper level boasted two separate terraces with a view overlooking the deep blue ocean.

The soft voice of the singer echoed through the mic and lovers held each other in their arms as they swayed to the music.

Quilt watched with admiration in his eyes. He loved the way she smiled when she was enjoying herself. The twinkle in her eyes, the curl of her lips. But then again, he loved just about everything about her. The only thing he hated was the way she would worry about things. The part of her that doubted that he would make heaven and earth move to make sure she was okay.

He took a sip of the glass of wine.

"I must be the luckiest guy in the world," he said. "Not many people have the chance at meeting a divine creature such as you. To meet their soul mate at the age of ten and still be in love with that person to this very day."

He was twenty-nine now, old enough to know that she was it. There would never be another.

Quilt thought about that one time in college that they had broken up for a year. Two different schools, two different states, they had been drifting apart. The bond that both had believed could never be broken had slowly become untangled due to the distance. He must have dated a number of girls but once he found out she was also dating someone else, he became livid, and he eventually became depressed. It was a very dark period in his early life and the consequences were far greater than he had expected. He drunk a lot, failed a few classes, and was on the verge of getting kicked out of school, and then the unthinkable happened. He was arrested for driving under the influence and she was the only person he had thought to call. Nothing had hurt him more than seeing the disappointment in her eyes that day she showed up to bail him out. It was a difficult period, though it was necessary. Until then, neither had quite understood the depth of love that existed between them, or the degree of difficulty in trying to move on without each other.

"So, what do you think?" She asked.

He had been lost in his memories and missed an entire conversation from his beloved.

"Yes," he answered, and as soon as the answer came out of his mouth, he realized he was in over his head. Knowing his wife, he had no doubt just agreed to partake in something crazy.

"Yay!" She squealed, clapping her hands in excitement. "I think we should go tomorrow. Parasailing looks like it is so much fun."

"Parasailing...." He echoed as he began to think about ways he could convince her to do an activity that was much safer. No way was he going to allow her to go gliding without adequate time to research the company. He had heard about too many cases that resulted in serious injuries because of faulty equipment.

"On second thought, I think we should wait. Remember! Dr. Cole said our chances for fertilization is better with no stress, and that includes no stressful activities."

"I hate it when you're right," she replied after mulling it over.

"I love it when you let me win," he smiled. "That pout in your lips makes me want to pull you across the table and kiss you right now."

"So, what's stopping you?" She grinned wickedly

"Well for one, that hot plate with lamb chops, and two, I'm afraid I'll break the two hundred dollars bottle of wine," he replied.

They both erupted in laughter. Hers like a waterfall. His was a deep rumble, the kind he felt in his lungs. Both echoing throughout the room.

The laughter continued late into the night over great conversation. And when they ate until they could not eat anymore, they danced the night away. Just two lovers slow dancing into the night.

It was late... 2am maybe even 3am. Time had escaped them due to all the fun they had been having. He lifted her so that she wouldn't have to walk the four steps leading to the villa.

He wanted her, not just to fulfill her dream of having a child, but he wanted her in a lustful, sinful way.

They had rarely made love frequently since her surgery and when they had, he had been so very tender and gentle. But this time he couldn't promise her a gentle experience because the night had set him ablaze. After all, the surgery had been months ago now. Something inside her was burning too. *Maybe it's my hormones*, she thought. Whatever it was, passion was involved.

"Undress me," she whispered.

"As you wish." He smirked as he unzipped her dress.

The red silk dress fell to the floor.

She stepped out of the dress and took another step closer to him until she was again pressed against his chest.

They kissed each other feverishly as her fingers searched for the buttons on his shirt.

One button down... then two. She searched for the third.

Impatiently she ripped the shirt open, her eyes admiring the firmness of his chest.

His fingers entangled in her hair as he pulled her head back, kissing her neck. There was a whimper in her throat and she felt her knees buckle.

He lifted her, drinking in her scent as he walked towards the bedroom where cries of pleasure erupted into the night.

The sun began its decent, casting a golden glow upon the water. There was a drop in the temperature that caused Dove to shiver as the crisp air reached her wet skin. The wind tussled her hair around. The beach was secluded and although she was grateful for the privacy, she did miss the sound of hearing children's laughter and watching them build sandcastles. She looked around the beach, taking in the view and basking in the silence which was soon filled by the squawking sound of sea gulls. They swooped through the sky, only diving down to catch fish. It was like poetry in motion.

There was another couple on the beach but further in the distance. She watched as another strolled along the warm sand, stooping to pick up treasures along the way.

She shivered again as the temperature dropped even further. She had nothing but her wet bathing suit and a beach towel that was now filled with sand wrapped around her.

Dove sat alone but her thoughts were filled with Quilt and the very special night they had. She couldn't help but hope that conception had occurred through all that magic. Her hand instinctively moved towards the center of her stom ach.

The tide was getting high and moving in closer. Dove gathered her things: A towel, a book and her sunglasses, and walked towards the villa.

"Quilt!" She yelled upon entering.

There no response. She walked inside of the bedroom, but he wasn't there.

He had mentioned having a few calls he needed to wrap up before promising to join her on the beach. The calls must have been more than a few because he never made it to the beach.

"Quilt!" she yelled one more time, making her way towards the balcony. Her eyes roamed the vast stretches of the beach, but he was nowhere in sight. There was nothing but sand, a few people, and the tall red and white lighthouse in the distance.

Dove picked up her cell phone and dialed his number. It rang a few times before she got an answer.

"Hey Love!"

"Where are you?" She asked.

He didn't answer the question. "Get dressed," he told her instead. "I'll pick you up in a few."

"Where are we going?"

"To dinner," he said. "Keep it simple."

She was still the most beautiful person he had ever laid eyes on. Her skin was always golden and smelled of an intoxicating mix of flowers with a playful hint of vanilla. Her hair, rich black and brown eyes, so shiny that if you looked long enough, you would feel like you're gazing at the stars.

She moved with the wind in her hair, walking towards him. She was gliding - almost as if she was floating on air.

He stood on the beach, both hands tucked into the pockets of his trousers.

What would I ever do without her, he thought.

She was his air, a necessity.

For her, it was the same.

On the beach, there was a nicely decorated table made of sand. Candles surrounded the rectangular table. Besides the light from the setting sun, two bamboo torches burned with dancing flames.

"Wow! I am thoroughly impressed, babe!" She glowed.

"Anything and everything for my Bird." He kissed her lips before they walked over to the table and sat on the bank of sand.

"You were always the creative one."

"Only when I have you as my inspiration," he replied.

The rest of the night passed with the sound of crashing waves against the shore. A silver moon provided light while the sun hid, and two kindred souls beamed at the stars above.

"I have a surprise for you," he told her.

"What!?" Dove exclaimed with excitement.

Quilt took her hand and lead her towards the board walk. As they walked along the sands, she noticed the paper cranes that illuminated the way. They were so many different colors... red... orange... pink... so many that she couldn't count.

"Quilt?" she asked, "Did you do this?"

"Yes." He nodded. "One of the benefits of marrying an architect," he smiled.

This was the single most romantic thing her husband had ever done.

He paused and before they stepped onto the board, he turned to face his wife.

"There is a legend that says if you can accomplish folding a thousand origami crane then one's wish will be granted. I started these a few weeks ago and finally finished today... a thousand of them... a thousand crane for you."

"Oh Quilt!" She cried and threw her arms around him.

"I have made a wish that your heart's deepest desire may be fulfilled... I can't tell you exactly what it is but we both know."

"Quilt Matthew." She cried as the water saturated her face. "You have taught me how to love before I was even old enough to recognize that I was in love. My greatest memories have you in all of them and now in this place and time, this will become the very memory I come back to when I need to feel your love."

"Grow old with me," he whispered.

"Forever and a day."

CHAPTER SIX

Ominous Sign

It was the last day of school and summer had officially began. Sunlight peaked through the window.

Quilt lay, sleeping like a baby. There was a fleeting moment when she thought about making a sick call in to work, just so she could sleep in next to him, but as quickly as the thought appeared, it vanished.

Today she would see her students off and would not see them for a couple of months. As much as she needed the time off, she also knew she would miss them dearly. Even the ones that made teaching a nightmare.

She pulled back the covers and slid from beneath the warmth of his arms. The coolness of the air-conditioned room made her shiver. Instinctively, Quilt pulled her back into the comfort of his arms. He would have the entire house freezing if he could, while she preferred it to be warm. They compromised, agreeing on sixty-eight degrees, although it was still too cool for her.

"Stay!" He mumbled under his breath, his eyes still shut. "Bird...Stay."

Her entire being would have liked nothing more than to stay wrapped up in his arms, but she did not want to disappoint a group of eight-year-olds who were looking forward to saying their goodbyes.

She kissed his sleepy eyelids.

"I wish I could, but then who would bring home the bacon?" She teased.

He chuckled, burying his face into the pillow, his grip tightening around her waist.

She struggled to loosen his hands but to no avail. It was like trying to remove a heavy mass from its gravitational pull.

The more her attempts failed, the louder his laughter. Until she was visibly frustrated and gave up. Quilt apologized for his playfulness and offered to get her to work on time. After all, at the speed he drove, he could have her there in less than twenty minutes.

She declined but welcomed the opportunity to lay in his arms just a bit longer.

"It's the last day of school." She kissed him gently on the lips. "There are no lessons to be taught, no tests, and no homework to be graded. Surely they wouldn't mind if I was fifteen minutes late." She continued to place small kisses on his lips. "Just fifteen minutes to make love to my adorable husband."

"I love the sound of that," Quilt said.

They had given up on all the planning and at trying so hard to conceive, both agreeing that it would happen if it was meant to be. They also agreed that adoption would be the next logical step. The most important thing was that they had each other.

The day was bittersweet. Dove had struggled to hold back the tears through her last goodbyes. She smiled, sending the students away for the long summer break. A few would be moving away. Even the horrible handwriting on the card made her somber, but at least her babies spelled every word correctly. A sweet sentimental note reminded her of how much she meant to her students and how much they meant to her as well.

They each hugged her on the way out, tightly wrapping arms around her as they made their way out the door.

She walked alongside the last student to the door of the main entrance, where she stood as she waved goodbye until they had all disappeared onto the school bus.

A chilling breeze began to blow. She looked up at the sky to see the dark clouds closing in. *A thunderstorm must be moving in*, she thought.

"Guess I should've listened to the weather this morning," she said out loud before turning to walk back to her class.

"Hey... we're meeting up at Charlie's for drinks in a few, are you in?" Karen asked.

She was the teacher in the class room across the hall. Karen was loud, bold and very much a straight shooter. A woman who had once admitted to almost running over her ex-husband with her car.

"I think it's about to rain pretty hard," Dove responded.

Karen's forehead wrinkled. "What rain?" she said, looking back towards the windows in her class room.

The sky was as clear as crystals and the sun glowed in all its glory.

"Bullshit!" She said in her very thick Bostonian accent. "If you don't want to hang with us then just say so." Her large round eyes suddenly seemed smaller.

"Karen I am not a bit afraid to tell you no," Dove's voice was stern. She was never fond of the way Karen would speak to people.

The workplace consensus regarding the two teachers was pretty much consistent across the board. Both were very opinionated and could hold their own, though Karen was a tad bit crazy, Dove was more rational and more pleasant to be around.

"Now..." she took a breath "I will gladly meet up at Charlie's for lunch."

"Perfect," Karen chuckled. "First drink is on me."

"...and Karen," she paused. "Please be on your best behavior or the first drink will definitely be on you in more ways than one."

Outside the air was laced with the smell of musk and the concrete surface felt as if it was overheating. Inside was a saving grace. Charlie's was unusually packed at this time of the day. There was an overwhelming smell of hot greasy fries, boisterous drunken men at the mahogany bar, all perched on their wooden stools, and the seasoned taste of heart disease as people stuffed a large amount of unhealthy food in their mouths.

The ladies sat in the green booth towards the back. It was closer towards the kitchen, so the aroma of fried onions lingered in the air. Of the five, Karen was the first to order drinks - a pitcher of New Orleans lemonade. Dove declined, opting instead to try a regular lemonade, much to Karen's disapproval. But Dove still had hopes of conceiving and so it had been awhile since she had tasted any alcohol, and besides it was only two o'clock. A tad bit too early by her drinking standards.

She listened as Karen talked about her ex, Camille bragged about her new luxury car, Mya slurped on her first drink, Jennifer told stories about her kids, and then Karen spoke some more about her ex.

"How is that fine husband of yours?" Asked Mya as she took bites of her mash potatoes.

"He is doing well. He just landed a contract to build the new state building downtown. We have the big dinner celebration tonight."

"Well that explain why you are not throwing back these alcoholic drinks with us," Camille laughed. "Partying hard tonight?"

"...and the fact that we are also trying to conceive." She added. She felt a sense of relief in sharing. She has always hidden the fact that they had difficulty conceiving, hiding behind lies that they just weren't ready. She had however just opened up the door for what felt like a hundred questions.

She breathed a sigh of relief when Karen started singing a song coming through the speakers, the rest knew the words and joined in merrily.

Another round of drinks, a few more bites of dessert, and a few more laughs at watching Karen deliver unsuccessful winks to the waiter.

"I really should get going," said Dove. She glanced at her watch before taking one last swig of her lemonade. The ice cube felt really soothing against her lips as she drained the last bit from the glass.

She removed two crisp twenty-dollar bills from her purse and placed it on the table.

"Yes," Karen said, motioning her hands towards the door. Her speech was slurred. "I need to leave as well."

"Am I the designated driver?" Karen grinned mischievously as she grabbed the car keys off the table.

"No, I am," Jennifer said as she snatched the keys from Karen's strong grip.

"That's a very wise decision," Dove added. "Bye ladies. Drive safely and let's meet up again over the summer."

They all agreed.

Outside the dark clouds were starting to reappear. She walked briskly towards her car as a tinkle of rain drops fell on her forehead. The wind felt cool against her skin. She loved the rain, always had, but the darkness in the clouds somehow made her afraid. She ran her fingers through her hair as to calm the unruly strands. The rolls of distant thunder were becoming more threatening. She glanced at the parking meter.

Good! She sighed. She still had fifteen minutes left.

She inserted her keys and got in the car, hoping the rain would ease, at least until she got home. As if traffic wasn't bad enough, the last thing she needed was crummy weather to add to it.

She peered through the rearview mirror and then the side view mirror before pulling out of her parking space.

The sound of something hitting her car startled her and she hit the brake hard in raw panic.

The screeching sound of a car behind her left her even more shaken. She sat with her foot still pressing heavy on the brakes, and her fingers tightly gripped the steering wheel.

"Lady, learn how to drive will you?" The heavy-set man hissed at her. He had now pulled up alongside her car and glowered at her through his beady eyes.

She heard him utter a few obscene words before driving off to the sound of horns blowing behind him.

Her hand found her throat and she gasped as she looked upon the bird that laid still against her windshield. She slowly pulled into the side of the road.

The rain began to pour but she knew she couldn't just leave that bird on her car, not like that... not when it laid there so helplessly.

She got out of the car, her hair now soaking wet, water dripped from her head and mingled with the salty tears running from her eyes. It looked like a sparrow and it was still alive. Its tiny legs twitched sporadically. She watched its chest rise and fall in a very shallow pattern.

It's suffering, she thought. But she didn't have enough courage to put it out of its misery.

Maybe she could save it? A vet could repair the injury, right? Or maybe the wildlife rehabilitators could save it?

The rain had eased... a few soft mists lingered.

She carefully removed the bird and inside the car, she gently placed it on a napkin while she frantically searched her phone for the wildlife sanctuary location.

Just then, Dove saw the rest of the teachers exiting the bar.

"Hey," she shouted through her car window. "Do you know where the wildlife center is located?"

They walked towards her car.

"I have an injured bird," Dove explained.

She removed the napkin to reveal its tiny legs that were still twitching.

"Let me see!" Karen held out her hand as Dove passed her the bird cuddled in the layers of paper.

"Oh...its suffering." Karen said, just before placing the birds head in between her fingers and swiftly snapping the bird's neck.

They all gasped.

"Karen, how could you!" Dove yelled in anger.

She handed the dead bird back to Dove. Its limp neck and bulging eyes that seemed to stare at her. "It needed mercy," Karen said before walking away.

CHAPTER SEVEN

In A Full Room

Quilt was standing by the bedroom door, his jawline visibly clenched. "Gosh, Bird," he said, "Do you know what time it is?"

She pushed past him to enter the bedroom. "Yes, Quilt and I'm sorry," she apologized as she removed her wet black slacks. She lifted the blue shirt above her head before walking into the bathroom.

"That's it?" He yelled, walking into the bathroom behind her. "No explanation. For goodness sake, it's after six... I don't think I have room to be late."

She turned the knob on the shower, the water drowning out the sound of his voice. The water ran over her head, washing the earthy smell from her skin. There were things she would rather forget... the sound of the bird hitting her windshield, the blood-stained glass, the way it gasped for air, and its final breath. The rain had disguised her tears much like the water from the showerhead was doing.

Quilt was silent for a moment - he was growing frustrated by her lack of accountability. Her apology quite frankly sounded insincere, as if she didn't care about going to the dinner.

He took a deep breath. "You know, you don't have to go."

"Quilt, I said I am sorry." Her voice was louder than she had intended, and she knew she had pissed him off further.

The shower curtains flew open, his eyes now filled with an intense gaze. "You knew about this event for weeks now, you could have said something earlier. Instead, you come home late, your mood sucks and you offer no explanation on why you're late."

She turned off the knob and stepped out of the bathtub, water dripping from her body.

Under any other circumstance, he would've stood back to admire her callipygous formation, but not today. Today, he was furious.

"Damn it Bird!" He shouted. He followed her into the bedroom. "The limo has been outside for the last twenty minutes. You could've called, texted... whatever. This was important to me!" The veins were visibly protruding from his forehead.

"I wanted to go!" She yelled back, screaming at the top of her lungs. "Shit happens!"

He threw his hands in the air. "Shit happens?" he repeated.

Quilt became silent as if he wanted to carefully select the next few words coming out of his mouth.

He ran his fingers through his hair before intertwining them on top of his head. "Never mind. Just stay!"

He grabbed the jacket to his tuxedo from the closet and made his way downstairs.

"Quilt!" she called out, but it was too late, he was already out the door.

She watched through the bedroom window as he entered the limo and she waited until she could no longer see the car in her view.

She just wasn't in the mood for a celebration tonight. She felt drained, besides, her hair was an utter mess. Then she thought about how superficial she was being. This was a big night for Quilt. She needed to be there, and so she pulled out the black dress she had planned on wearing. She blow dried her hair then added a braided ponytail. Quickly doing her make-up, then adding her favorite pair of earrings. She was amazed that she was out the door in less than sixty minutes.

There was a long walk from the parking garage to the Epic Conventional Center. The air smelled of the pleasant dewy petrichor of the post rain.

She walked swiftly but stealthily towards the entrance.

She stood with her back against the wall, unsure which table she should be sitting at. From a distance she watched, proudly, as Quilt made his way towards the podium on stage.

The palm of her hands hurt from clapping so hard.

"Thank you... thank you," Quilt smiled.

"Oh wow!" he said. "Thank you to everyone. I am truly overwhelmed." He took a deep breath before continuing. "Please everyone, have a seat." He motioned his hand.

Dove continued to clap and then she placed her two middle fingers in her mouth, creating a high-pitched whistling sound.

Real classy, she told herself.

Her husband, however, found it amusing, or maybe he was just overjoyed by the sight of her being there.

"...and thank you to my beautiful whistleblower in the back." He gave her a thumbs up.

She in return made her hands into the shape of a heart.

He looked great up there, possibly the most handsome creature she had ever laid eyes on. She listened as he thanked his team for helping to secure what was quite possibly the biggest contract of his career. Quilt had rehearsed his speech at least ten times, and she had listened each time, but in this moment, she felt as if she was hearing it for the first time. She had also discovered something new about the man she had known most of her life. He was a natural in the spotlight. All this time she was sure he would've been a nervous wreck, and here he was, smiling and enjoying himself as if he had done it numerous times before. It was one of the proudest moments in her life.

"In a room full of a million people, I would still find you because you would be the only one that shines." Quilt whispered in her ear. "Thanks for showing up." He didn't tell her, but he knew she would be there.

CHAPTER EIGHT

The Unthinkable

"Dove?" The voice was shaky on the other end.

"Yes?" Dove responded. "Raven what's wrong?" she asked as fear slowly crept its way inside.

There was a pause, but she knew Raven was still there. She could still hear an elevator ding and voices in the background.

"You're scaring me!" Dove continued.

Raven took a deep breath. "Where are you?" She asked, ignoring all of Dove's previous questions.

"I'm driving. A bit of traffic but I will be on Farmington Avenue in a few."

"She's on Farmington," she overheard Raven whispering to someone.

"That's good... you're close." Raven sounded relieved. "I need you to come to Southside Hospital."

A few scenarios bombarded Dove's mind but only one made sense. Her heart began to race.

"Is it mom?" She yelled.

Her mother had suffered a small stroke after her father died and with her mother going into her private work practice, she knew another was inevitable.

"Dove, the doctors are here to speak with me. Just please drive safe I'll fill you in when you get here."

And then Raven was gone. The dial tone continued to beep over the Bluetooth car device as she reminded herself to remain calm, which was unsuccessful.

A frazzled Dove made a sharp left on Woodbury. Someone flipped her the finger when she impatiently blew the horn after they had lingered at a green light for a bit.

She flipped her finger back in retaliation as she sped through the intersection.

The parking lot was practically full. She managed to squeeze her way between a minivan and a pickup truck.

She grabbed her bag and made a dash towards the entrance.

Her heart was beating a mile per minute. She prayed her mother was just fine - that maybe Raye had overreacted.

She had told her a hundred times to retire, it's not like she needed the money. Dad had made sure they were well off.

Plus, it was a widely known fact that Psychiatrists are plagued with a stressful job.

Dove approached the information desk. An older lady greeted her with a smile. Her glasses rested on the brim of her nose. She reminded Dove of her fifth-grade school teacher, the one who had inspired her to also become one.

She glanced at her name badge: Fancy Butt.

And for a second, she was able to find humor as she laughed silently, thankful that Fancy was from a different era because hers would've roasted her mercilessly.

"How can I help you?" She asked politely. Her voice was hoarse as if she was former smoker - maybe even still one. Looking at her skin it was evident, with its haggard and wrinkled appearance.

"Hi. I'm trying to locate my mother - Elaine Williams." Dove responded. Her legs twitched impatiently as Fancy scrolled through her records.

She whispered a small prayer.

In her heart, she just knew it had to be another stroke.

She had already watched the heart disease strip her of her grandmother and her great-grandmother.

She had hoped her mother was free but now it appeared it had struck again.

"I'm sorry ma'am but I don't see an Elaine Williams?" Fancy said.

Dove shook her head. "No... no... no! Please check again. My sister said she was here," she argued. "What about her date of birth? Could you locate her that way?"

She rubbed her forehead, she could feel the headache coming in.

"Sure dear, I'll try." Fancy replied, lacking enthusiasm.

"Dove!" Robyn yelled as she exited the elevator with Raven at her side.

Dove breathed a sigh of relief.

"Never mind," she told Fancy, and she thanked her for her assistance.

She walked briskly towards her sisters. Her eyes searching their faces for a sign that things were okay.

"I'm sorry but I came as quickly as I could," she apologized.

Robyn hugged her tightly. "We will be here for you." She said softly.

She sounded almost sympathetic. *But why would she sympathize with me?* Dove wondered. It was her mother too and besides, she hated pity.

Robyn wiped the tears from her eyes and then she stepped back, allowing Raven to step in.

Raven's eyes were red, her cheeks markedly stained with traces of white crystals.

"Raye, where is she?" Dove asked. "Was it another stroke?"

"No Dove." Raven shook her head. "It's..." her voice trembled, and she struggled with getting the words out.

Dove's heart plunged deeper into her chest. She felt lightheaded and she feared the worst... she had been too late. She was gone!

Her mouth hung open. It was as if she had taken a hard blow to her chest - knocking every bit of air from her lungs.

"I need... water," she said. Her voice cracked, and her legs barely got her to the other side of the vending machine.

"What the hell is going on Raye?" Robyn yelled under her breath. "You told her it was mom?"

"She was driving Robyn. I didn't have time to correct her."

"Well, we have to tell her before she gets to that room!"

"Tell me what?" Dove asked. She twisted the cap off the bottled water and took a few sips to ease the burning dryness in her throat.

"Dove... sweetie." Robyn began as she rubbed her sister's shoulder. She had promised herself to be strong for Dove, her younger sister would need her. But it all became too much, strength had failed her, and her lips began to quiver.

"She's gone, isn't she?" Dove swiped at the wetness from her nose.

"Well, no. It's not..." Raven spoke softly.

"Then what!" Dove screamed which garnered certain stares in their direction. "What are you two not telling me?"

"Let's have a seat."

It only infuriated Dove some more, and she unleased a few explicit words at Robyn's suggestion.

"It's not mom, Dove... it's Quilt!"

"Quilt?" she asked "Quilt is in Philadelphia. This doesn't make sense..."

"He was coming home early. He wanted surprise you." Robyn explained. "He called me this morning and asked me to keep you out until around six. At least that was the plan." Robyn sobbed. His limo was hit head on by a truck. The driver was killed instantly. Quilt is still fighting."

Dove gasped... what was this she was feeling? It was as if an elephant was standing on her chest. She couldn't breathe. She needed air.

She felt it... the spinning... the bottle slipping from her hand, and then darkness.

"Dove... Dove!" She heard someone shout.

It was all a dream or, so she hoped. Dove opened her eyes to the unfamiliar tan colored wall.

Her back ached and she braced her arms to sit up. Her hand felt the cold from the metal frames on the bed.

She grimaced on feeling a spasm in her neck when she turned her head to survey the room.

"Ouch!" She whimpered.

"Good," you're awake. "Your sisters are in the waiting room. I'll get them," a man said, and before she could ask any questions, he had disappeared from the room.

Robyn, in her usual dramatic mode, was the first to enter. Dove stared at her sister's messy raccoon eyes. She knew something was terribly wrong. The Robyn she knew would die before she let anyone see her like this – runny makeup, shirt untucked, hair as wild as the wind.

She laughed at her sister's appearance as she walked into the room.

"Dove, do you know where you are?" Robyn's head tilted to the side as she tried to make sense of Dove's strange mood.

Dove shook her head as she tried to put the bits and pieces together.

She remembered the hospital, her mom, Quilt, and something about an accident.

Then it all came back to her, like waves crashing against the shore.

She jumped from the bed and she staggered backward before launching forward, her escape blocked by Raven.

"How long have I been out?"

"Twenty minutes."

"I need to see him," she pleaded.

And without hesitation, they obliged.

Quilt is still fighting. The words replayed in her head.

He was still alive. This she was sure. If he was gone she would've known... she would've felt it.

He will be alright. She tried to convince herself.

They stepped into the crowded elevator. Each girl took their place in the center of the tiny space. A tall grey-haired gentleman pressed the button on the silver panel each time someone shouted out their designated floor. Thoughts of Quilt flooded Dove's mind and anxiety seeped in like water through a cracked wall.

She wanted to cry, and no sooner than a teardrop had appeared, it was quickly brushed away by the lady that bumped her on her way out onto the fifth floor. She was dressed in dark clothing and Dove began to wonder what her story was... she wondered about the stories of all the people in the elevator. Were they like her? Were their loved ones fighting too? Or was she pretty much the only one that was suffering this deep?

As she stepped out onto the sixth floor, she was immediately overpowered by the recognizable smell.

It wreaked of rubbing alcohol and menthol, much like her grandmother's cabinet.

And then her eyes were wet again.

The sounds made her uneasy, beeping at her in all directions. Everything scared her, the machines, the people in white coats, and the lady in the hall, running towards an erratic sound.

She came upon the entrance to Quilt's room and paused before exchanging her shallow breaths for much deeper ones.

"Just remember he needs you to be strong," Raven said. She wanted so desperately to tell her it was okay, but she knew better. It really wasn't okay. It was terrible.

Dana saw her standing in the doorway. She had been at her only child's bedside since she had received the call.

She gathered herself from her praying position. Her eyes were bloody red, and water coursed down her cheeks.

"Bird." She walked over to hug her. She was the only other person beside Quilt and her school friends to consistently call her as such. It made her miss hearing his voice now even more.

Just the thought of the possibility of never hearing him say it ever again made her heart leap.

Dana gripped her tightly. "He's still here," she whispered. "I didn't raise a quitter." She pulled firmly at Dove's chin to look her in the eyes.

Dove nodded to let her know she understood.

"Can you give me a moment alone with him?"

Her sisters hesitated before freeing her hand.

Both knew that there was nothing they could do to prepare Dove for what she was about to see. They had only hoped to be her source of comfort for when she needed them.

Dana stepped aside and allowed Dove to walk inside of the room. She shivered as she stepped inside. *The thermostat must be set at freezing, or maybe it's just my nerves,* She thought.

Dana took another glance in her son's direction before closing the door behind her to allow Dove time with Quilt.

"Quilt?" Dove whispered softly as she took a few steps closer to the bed.

His body was still, motionless, and his face almost unrecognizable. It was swollen and discolored. The kind of color that combined the flames of fire with the deepest blue of the ocean.

She gasped and covered her mouth to silence her wail as she remembered something from her father's coma. The nurse had told her that the hearing was the last of the senses to leave.

Quilt could hear her and the last thing she wanted was for him to hear her cry.

Her hand clutched her grandmother's silver cross that dangled from her neck.

She removed her hand from her mouth to exhale and her tongue tasted the saltiness of her tears. Her lungs burned, oh how they felt like fire.

So many machines.

Why?

She took his hand. It felt like an icicle.

The monitor above the bed started to beep. There were waves and then a series of spikes.

"Yes baby. I'm here."

Dove watched as the rate climbed.... one-hundred... one-hundred and ten... one-hundred and twenty.

She couldn't tell if it was good or bad, but she knew his heart was beating.

She took his hand and brought it to her lips.

The numbers slowed... one-hundred... ninety... eighty-nine.

* * *

"You're bleeding," Dove said out loud upon noticing a bag hanging from the bedside. A crimson colored substance trickled slowly into the bag. And there it was again... the feeling of being alone in deep murky water, suddenly feeling like you're about to drown.

"He was," a voice behind her clarified.

The voice was soft, almost angelic.

"He had a lot of internal bleeding. He fractured his skull, ruptured his spleen and damaged both his kidneys," she stated. She extended her hand and Dove shook it lightly.

"I'm Doctor Henson."

Dove stood silently, then cries escaped her lips. They had never left, she had just managed to contain them. This time, she just couldn't, and the sobbing came with intermittent pauses each time she tried to recover from the pain in her chest.

It felt has if someone had reached down into the depths of her soul and was punching her repeatedly.

Quilt didn't deserve this.

She was the one who had lit that house on fire... the one who stole the expectant mother's parking spot... the one who cursed like a sailor.

Not Quilt! He was good... and giving. Why him? Why not her?

"His heart is strong though... it stopped twice during surgery but each time he fought his way back," the doctor continued. "We managed to stop the bleeding and that's a huge step in the right direction."

"So, what's next?" Dove asked.

Doctor Henson smiled. "Mrs. Mathew, this is probably the most difficult part... but now we wait and see."

One scenario flooded her mind, then it was followed by another and another, until it became too painful to think.

She had heard the same thing about her father and sadly he succumbed to his illness.

The doctor was right... the waiting can be the most difficult part.

"...and we pray," Dove said.

Dr. Henson's lips curled slightly. She had much admiration for hope but unfortunately, she had seen too many families end up hurt and disappointed on the account of hope.

She couldn't know anyone beliefs, but she was a woman of science. Science had given Quilt Matthew less than a week to live.

She removed the vibrating pager from her side. Her brows scrunched together as she reviewed the message.

"I have to run but please... let me know if you have any questions."

Dove watched as her small frame exited the door.

Quilt was in a pretty bad shape, even she had to admit that, but what she had not imagined, nor could she ever fathom, was being in this world without him.

So, she held on to hope. It was her only way of surviving.

* * *

Dove took a seat in the chair by his bed. She felt lost and alone.

She held onto Quilt's hand for comfort.

"Where's Dove?" She heard her mother's voice in the hall.

She could hear Robyn asking her to lower her voice.

Then she heard the door creaking and Mrs. Williams walked in. Her cashmere coat sweeping the floor.

The smell of gardenia and lilac overpowered the room.

"Oh Quilt." Mrs. Williams cried, and she gently brushed her hand across his face.

"Dove. Honey, I wish I had gotten here sooner but traffic was horrible."

She hugged her daughter tightly and Dove wept in her arms.

Sometimes, nothing feels safer than a mother's embrace.

Dana made her way back in the room. Not much had changed. She still looked like hell. Dana too, held her daughter-in-law.

Raven and Robyn stood closely behind her. And for a while, the family sat in silence. Everyone holding on to someone.

They held each other until two nurses entered the room, both looked like they were having a rough day.

The one with the messy bun respectfully requested a few minutes with Quilt, to perform care. The family exited the room, though Dove was reluctant to leave his side.

But Dove promised Quilt that she would never be too far away from his side and she waited by the door until the nurse's tasks were completed.

CHAPTER NINE

Don't Let Go!

"I need twenty of epinephrine," one of the doctors yelled.

"Epinephrine!" the nurse repeated as she handed her the syringe.

"Nothing on the monitor!" another shouted.

"Debrillator at 200."

"All clear," someone yelled.

Dove stood by the door. She had been forcedly removed from the room but managed to steal peaks through the slight crack in the door.

"Quilt don't leave... don't leave," she prayed.

This was the second time his heart had stopped since she had been at the hospital. A week later and they said there were no improvement, but she had not left his side. Her family took turns providing her with food and clothing. Raven had volunteered to stay at the house while Dove remained with Quilt.

Dove watched the paddles hit his chest again, sending his body into a series of jolts. Every pound, every shock... she could feel. Fear had paralyzed her, and she was too frightened to even cry.

"Baby don't go," she pleaded once more.

"Sinus," the man in light blue scrubs yelled out.

She breathed a sigh of relief. She had come to learn that sinus meant something good, but she had hung around long enough to know that there were other factors that also mattered.

Then she heard the most beautiful sound that had become her source of comfort. The beeping on the heart monitor. His heart was beating steadily. She finally unfroze long enough to let a lone tear roll from her eye. Dana had gone to the chapel to pray. Inside of Dove's pocket was her cell phone. She called to give Dana the good news, who repeated a series of praises.

Dove waited patiently for her turn to enter the room. There must have been at least ten people that exited the small room. Dr. Harvey had been working the morning shift. He was the last to exit. Unlike Dr. Henson, his demeanor was stern and mostly cold. His hands were tucked in his immaculate white coat as he slowly approached her.

He removed one hand and motioned to have a word with her. And for a quick second she thought she recognized a softness that crossed his face. She had never seen the man smile and even if he did, it would've been hidden by the thick mustache that lined his upper lip. She wondered what in his experience could've made him so aloof.

She followed behind as he led her to a private room.

"Mrs. Matthew," he addressed her. "I know my colleagues have mentioned this before, but have you given any more thought about signing the do not resuscitate orders?"

"There's nothing to think about Dr. Harvey," she said with conviction. "I believe my husband will recover from all of this."

He folded his arms. "His heart has stopped a total of four times. Each day he gets weaker. It has been almost two weeks and we have seen no improvement." He paused at the realization that his voice had escalated.

"Mrs. Mathew..." he sighed deeply. "We just can't keep sticking paddles on his chest."

"My husband is alive and breathing," she yelled a little louder than intended.

He shook his head. "I hate to sound callous and cold, but it's the machine that is breathing for him."

He paused for a moment at what he saw. In front of him was a woman who was in love and consumed by fear. A woman who would possibly drown in sorrow. It made him thankful that he had never known such a love.

His tone got softer as he explained, "I understand that this is an extremely difficult time for you, but as a doctor, it's also my duty to do what is best for my patients. The pressure on his brain is increasing, his heart is giving out... and he just wouldn't survive another surgery."

Dove was silent as she tried to process all the information he had thrown at her.

"I don't want you to decide now... only you know best, what your husband would've wanted."

Dr. Harvey moved closer to the door.

Dove sat down on the sofa. She had to catch her breath. She inhaled then exhaled a few times, closing her eyes in the process, forcing back her tears.

She saw Quilt. She could see his round smooth baby face. He had on a blue and grey striped shirt with a rounded collar. It was a Ralph Lauren. It brought out the beautiful brown in his eyes.

She had complimented him on the shirt which made him blush.

"Oh, this old thing!" he smiled. He was always so modest.

He was thirteen. They had been throwing rocks from across the street at Miss Clarkson's Pit-bull. His name was Trigger, who by the fourth rock and grown frustrated and somehow escaped the gate. She remembered them being chased by the huge, angry dog and them running for dear life. Quilt was in front, his long-legs had always given him the advantage, yet he had slowed so she would be in front of him. He was the first to make it up the tall Oak tree.

"Bird! Take my hand," he shouted.

She remembered losing focus. Terrified as Trigger was at her feet.

"Bird," Quilt shouted again. "I got you." He helped pull her to safety.

"Don't let go," she pleaded as Trigger nipped at her heels.

"I won't," he promised.

They would sit in that big Oak tree until the sun had set.

"Dr. Harvey," she said. "I don't need to think about it anymore. I believe Quilt is holding on, his heart keeps trying to find its way back."

He paused in the doorway.

"But Mrs. Matthew, what if he is actually trying to leave... and we keep bringing him back?" he said solemnly.

* * *

It had been four uneventful days. Although Quilt's conditioned had not improved, it also had not worsened.

Winter was cold, possibly the coldest one yet and she was happy to be wrapped up in her blue oversized sweater, outside looked awfully bitter. She watched through the window on the sixth floor as the powdery fluff fall towards the ground. People watching had become one of her past times during her stay. A lady gripped her scarf tightly as it started to blow with the wind. She could hear the howling against the window pane. A cloud of air escaped the mouths of two people having a conversation by a lamp post. The light bulb from the street light on the corner flickered a few times before going out. Sunlight had been replaced by the dim light of the moon and grey clouds now found their meeting place in the night sky.

Ten more days and it would be Christmas. She despised winter, yet Christmas was her favorite time of the year. It was Quilt's also.

"His heart is getting weaker." The doctor's words echoed inside of her head and they made her shiver more than the cold temperature in the room. She hugged herself tightly and rubbed her hands against the goosebumps on her arms. The thought of her husband not being there for the holiday sent a chill up and down her spine.

She walked over and stood at Quilt's bedside. She'd always admired his deep-set brown eyes. There was an ache in her heart and she longed to see them.

"Quilt," she whispered. "I believe I'm doing what is best for you." She sniffled. "...but I never want you to hurt in any way. I just wish you could come back and talk to me."

She wiped her eyes with the sleeve of her sweater but as quickly as she wiped them away, more tears would come, until her lashes were heavy with water.

A rhythmic beat was coming from the one of the machines and it was loud enough to send two nurses rushing into the room.

"High pressure alarm!" one said to the other as she checked the machine.

She thought she saw a look of relief on their faces. They both appeared to be so young. Twenty-two...twenty-three perhaps.

"Is there anything I can get for you Mrs. Matthew?" one of the nurses asked after they had thoroughly reset the machine. They all seemed to have pity in their voice, or maybe it was empathy. She was sure in their mind she was already a widow.

"No... but thank you," she replied politely.

She just needed to rest. She pulled up the small chair, rested her head against the bedrail and closed her eyes, maybe for minute.

* * *

Eyelids flickered. Her heartbeat was steady. Slow, deep breaths. Dove had entered an R.E.M state of sleep.

She was standing on a vessel, a ship. It rocked from side to side as waves was sent crashing on the side. She wasn't alone, there were a large group of people who seemed oblivious to the gigantic waves. They were busy enjoying themselves and they reeked of rum and cigars. Her eyes were drawn to the tall frame at the starboard side of the ship. His back was turned towards her and he appeared to be watching the waves.

"Quilt?" She questioned.

"Quilt!" she yelled, waving her hands in the air in the hope that he would see her amongst the crowd.

He turned around to smile and then he went back to face the roaring sea.

Dove's eyes grew large at the sight of the oncoming wave. It was the largest one she had ever seen, and it was headed straight for Quilt. She shouted his name, and everything felt like it was in slow motion, even her sprint towards him.

The wave hit the side of the ship and sent her flying across the deck. She heard a thump as her head connected with the rail on the ship. The pain felt like someone had inserted a long sharp knife through her skull.

Dove scraped herself off the wet floor, stood tall-straightened her shoulders and planted her bare foot firmly on the floor. Her hands lifted the hem of her long white dress that was now drenched with the smell of sulfur and brine.

She ran but another wave would soon toss her around like a child. The ship would roll and yaw like a rollercoaster, so this time, she told herself she would crawl. She crawled past the passengers who still seemed to be enjoying themselves.

A strong wind started to force her back, but she had determination. Dove moved towards the hand rail and gripped it tightly, pulling her way towards Quilt until her hands bled. He held onto her and kissed her like he hadn't seen her in a while, soaking in the saltiness of her lips.

She felt safe in his arms, though she begged him to seek shelter.

He told her he wasn't afraid.

But she was... she was petrified.

Above, dark clouds scattered across the never-ending sky. While below, the wind was spinning the water like a mixture in a blender, sending a tumultuous wave that charged towards the air. Through her heavy soaked lids, she peaked at the sky. The clouds smiled mockingly.

She heard the waves clap louder as if they were pleased by their performance and felt her grip on him loosen as the wind started forcing her back.

"You have to let go." he mouthed and he kissed her hand.

She slid further as she desperately tried to grab him like a drowning woman grasping at a straw.

"No Quilt!" she screamed, and she watched helplessly as he climbed aloft the sail.

"Bird, I got you," he said before jumping into the torrid water that suddenly became calm.

She felt her body jerk. She sat up in the chair after the realization that she had been dreaming.

"'I'm sorry, I didn't mean to startle you," the nurse apologized. "I was trying to be quiet in switching these canisters."

She watched as the nurse held the container filled with serosanguinous drainage from the tube coming from Quilt's chest.

"It's okay. I probably need to move to the recliner anyways. This small chair is way too uncomfortable," she smiled.

The nurse programmed machines, switched tubes and administered medications all under Dove's probing eyes. She seemed skilled, much older than all his previous nurses.

When she was done, she smiled at Dove. "You know, some of us medical folks like to get technical and say that death occurs when the brain is no longer functioning and then there are those of us that believe..." She raised her hand, "...that as long as there is a beating heart, there is a soul still fighting." She gently pat Dove on her shoulder, "...but I'm an old woman who also believe that death isn't final. Hang in there, honey," she smiled before leaving the room.

At six o'clock in the morning an exuberant Dana walked through the door. She reminded her so much of her mother: Both loved making an entrance, though her mother was a little less dramatic. She wondered why the two had not enjoyed each other's company more, maybe the religion factor played a bigger barrier than Dove had thought. Elaine relied heavily on scientific facts. Dana on the other hand, relied heavily on faith, which was the reason for her positive attitude in the last couple of days.

According to Dana, she had seen the signs that Quilt was going to be alright or as she had put it, "The Angels spoke to her."

In her hand was a paper tray, two cups of hot chocolate and one vanilla chai. The hot chocolates were for her and Dana, and the chai was for Quilt, only because he loved the smell of it.

She placed the cup on his bedside table and lifted the lid. The aroma of vanilla and cinnamon swirled around the room, lingering in the air just above his bedside.

"Bagel?" she asked Dove.

"Yes, I'll have one after I freshen up."

"That reminds me... I brought fresh clothes for you. Give me a few and I'll grab them from the car."

Dove dragged herself from the comfort of the recliner. Her back ached a little and she wished she could be back sleeping in the comfort of her own bed, but not without Quilt.

Dana hugged her and placed a kiss on her cheek. Her eyes roamed over her daughter in law's small frame.

"I think you should have two bagels. You're starting to look very frail."

"One will be just fine Dana," she smiled politely.

She knew she had lost weight, but she really hadn't been eating much.

"I guess stress will do that to you," she said softly as she forced a half smile.

"Why don't you get out the hospital today? Maybe browse some of the shops or you could go to the chapel?" She brushed strands of hair away from Dove's face.

Her voice was saturated with deep concern upon seeing that Dove had not once left the unit.

"Thanks for the offer but Dana you know I don't go any further than the elevator."

"I know Dove. You're my daughter too and I just want you to be okay."

"...and I will be," she assured her before heading into the bathroom.

She pondered whether to tell Dana about the dream but decided it was best not to do so. The dream had left her feeling uneasy and she still needed to figure out what it all meant.

They drank hot chocolate, ate bagels with strawberry cream cheese and read words from some of Quilt's favorite poets.

The day had seemed to fly by, maybe because it was filled with so many visitors throughout the day... cousins, friends, co-workers. Quilt's dad had made his third visit from New York and each time Dana had made a mad dash out of the room. The divorce had not ended amicably. He walked away free to be with his mistress, while Dana had walked away with a whole lot of money.

"That's what the bastard deserved," she had uttered on more than one occasion.

He sat in the chair next to Quilt, unaware of the admiring eyes examining his every move. Dove was always fond of the way Frank Matthew shared not only his looks but much of the same mannerisms as his son. They walked the same and both did the same thumb twiddle when they were nervous. Frank even shared the same left handedness as Quilt.

She remembered a time, before the divorce, how close the two were. Their bond was a solid thing, and then the separation happened, and the young boy felt he had to choose sides. He had blamed his father for breaking his family apart and although it took some time, the two had worked things out.

Visitors came and left throughout the day leaving Dove alone by Quilt's side. She stared at Quilt, lying in the bed, watching as his chest slowly rose and fell. He seemed at peace, and she wondered if he was really without pain.

"Quilt?" She lifted his flaccid arm. "Are you okay, my love?" Dove paused as if she was awaiting a response. "I know we promised each other never to be selfish, but that dream I had last night..." She took a moment to swallow the bitter taste of her next few words, "were you telling me to let you go?" she asked.

"I don't want you to leave me but then again, I don't want you to ever suffer... that's not the way we love." Her voice started to crack, revealing the fear she so desperately tried to hide by pretending to be brave and strong. "I loved that you visited me in my dream. It was nice seeing you smile and even holding you felt so real. Visit me again my love." She kissed him goodnight.

CHAPTER TEN

Mercy

"There's a storm rolling in," one of the nurses warned.

Dove had been so disconnected from the outside world. She barely even watched television any more.

"Well that explains the dark cloudy sky at this time of the day," Dove replied.

Four more days until Christmas. She should have been feeling excited, but the doctors had given her more bad news.

Quilt's heart had been beating more erratically. They now had to add another medication to see if it would help. Dove thought about the uphill battles her husband had fought through. She ached for each time they had shocked his heart. She thought about the many tubes that seemed to be hanging out of every orifice, the machines... and she knew. Quilt wouldn't have wanted to live like this. That was why a very tearful Dove told her husband that she would understand if he couldn't stay.

"He won't leave while you're watching," a voice said from behind her.

Mrs. Williams entered the room, a brown catering bag in her hand.

"Hey mom," Dove mustered up enough facial muscles to give a faint smile.

Her mother pulled a few tissues from her Chanel purse and wiped her daughter's tears, a single tear glistening in the corner of her very own eye.

"I remember when your dad was ill. I was with him the entire day. The minute I left to get coffee, the man decides to take his very last breath. I returned, and he was already gone, he didn't have the heart to tell me goodbye," she laughed ruefully. "Men and their stupid pride. I believe they see it as their weakest moment. Something they never want us women to see. Isn't that right, Quilt?" she asked, placing a kiss on his cheek.

An hour passed, and they sat silently next to him. Dove read him Dickens' Great Expectations and when she had finally finished, she softy rested her head against his chest in the way he adored.

"Mom, do you think I can have a few minutes alone with Quilt?" she asked. "And then we can test this theory of yours," she said somberly, "we can go get coffee."

Mrs. Williams nodded. She hugged Quilt. "I will always love you," she whispered in a way that felt like goodbye.

Dove had decided and maybe Quilt had decided too, but she prayed her theory was very wrong. Dove whispered softly in Quilt's ear. She said everything that she wanted to say. She wanted him to know that he had been her entire life, how proud she was to be his wife. She apologized for not being able to give him a child, and for every argument that she had caused.

She whispered many things and she wanted to tell him and so many other things, as if he didn't already know. And then she told him one final thing before she left, "I will meet you in summer, my eternal flame."

The thunder boomed and echoed across the sky. Flashes of lightning lit up the darkness like a shooting show of fireworks. The wind screamed as it vigorously tossed around stop lights hanging from its cables. The halls were empty. Mrs. Williams saw the storm that had desolated the area as she peered out one of the windows in the hall.

Dove stood by the elevator. She was shaking like a nervous wreck. She nodded her head before resting it on her mother's shoulder. Mrs. Williams placed her arm around her, guiding her into the lift. Dove's eyes followed every button on the descent. Panic was starting to set in. She exhaled through pursed lips as she really tried to grasp the possible implications of her decision. A life without Quilt was just impossible.

"Mom!" she yelled "Let's go back... I don't want coffee."

"What?" Mrs. Williams spoke softly. Not that she blamed her daughter, but she wanted Dove to be sure.

"I want to be selfish. I don't like your theory. I hate coffee," she rambled.

The elevator stopped at the lobby and Mrs. Williams pushed the button to the sixth floor. It began to ascend when they heard it. The overhead announcement blasted again. "Code Blue. Code Blue!"

Dove knew. She felt it in her heart, a deep pain seeped into her chest. In the pit of her stomach she felt a feeling beyond fear. Her last words to him started to regurgitate into her mouth and she tried suppressing the gagging triggered by regret. She knew the code was for Quilt and she needed to get to him. She needed to stop him from leaving.

The elevator stopped on the fourth and then on the fifth. Her anxiety only grew, and she wondered what supernatural forces were interfering with her getting where she was needed.

And then when the door finally opened on the sixth, Dove made a mad dash leaving her mother to follow behind.

She ran as fast as she could and with every breath her lungs burned. She pushed the door to his room and her sight immediately searched the overhead monitor for the waves that had once brought her comfort.

There were no beeps. No spikes.

He was gone, like the days of summer.

Taking with him the warmth she had needed to survive. Winter had come, and it was cold. Death was not some heroic figure that had just rescued a comatose man, sparing him from pain; he was a coward, a thief who had not only snatched the soul of the dying, but would rob the living of every vital breath in her body.

Her lungs screamed for air and pain pierced through her chest like a knife, forcing her to bend at the knees. She surrendered and then she allowed the tears to break free like an avalanche. The weight on her chest was far too heavy and cries escaped her lips. Like shards of glass, they pierced through the ears of the sympathetic onlookers in the room. They were the kind of cries that elicit agony in the individual observer.

"We'll give you some time alone," Dr. Henson spoke, prompting the staff to clear the room.

"I'm so sorry for your loss." the last nurse apologized with tears in her eyes.

Her cries echoed into the hall before they were muffled into her mother's chest.

"I need to see him," she whimpered. She couldn't believe that he was really gone. She tried to stand but her legs failed her. She had no more strength left. Mrs. Williams assisted her daughter to her knees. Dove glanced at the window and it was raining mercilessly. She felt his skin, she kissed his lips softly, all the while praying that her kiss could bring about a fairytale ending.

Dove whispered his name and then after the pregnant silence she cried "Quilt." She echoed as she trembled through sobs, "you let go!"

Mrs. Williams had just lost a son. The little boy she knew from next door had left this world and he would take a piece of everyone's heart with him. She thought about Dana and she dreaded that she would have to make a call about a mother's worst nightmare. She wrapped an arm around her daughter and gently rubbed her tense shoulders. Dove sunk deeper into the warmth of her mother's embrace.

"When I lost your father, one of the nurses told me about a tradition in her country. She said they would open up a window, so the soul could leave and find their way to heaven." Mrs. Williams spoke softly and was careful with her words. "I think it's time you opened the window for Quilt."

Dove walked towards the window, pausing on each step that would take her closer to setting free a soul that she felt belonged to her.

She unlocked the window and pushed it open as the sudden gust of wind struck her in the face. It scattered her hair before grabbing the strands to strike her in the face. She held the window open until the wind forced it shut.

Dove closed her eyes, inhaling deeply. She took a few steps back as she stared at the dark skies through the window.

"I just felt him leave." She sniffled into the top of her shirt then her sleeves. "Mom," she cried, "I felt him leave."

She walked briskly over to where her mother was standing and lifted her arm to her face "Here," she said, "It smells of leather and citrus."

"Yes." Mrs. Williams' smile was thin, and she eyed Dove with a pained sympathetic face. Whatever her daughter needed, she vowed she would be there to help. She had decided it would be done, and the vault she had locked away with her tears became open as she cradled her daughter in her arms once more.

CHAPTER ELEVEN

When Dove Cry

"Breathe!" Raven pleaded. The cordless phone lay beeping on the floor.

"Dove open your eyes," she yelled as she pressed against her sister's chest. Her arms were weary with fatigue and with each push, she begged God to give her the strength to do another.

She counted to thirty, blew two breaths into Dove's mouth and repeated the process until she heard the loud screeching noise from vehicles outside. It comforted her.

A red and blue light flashed through the window pane and danced erratically along the wall.

"Hold on. They're here!" she said.

Dove's frail body laid still on the wet wooden floor. Her damp skin smelled of English rose petals and her hair dripped of her bath water.

Raven blew her final breath and lifted herself to her knees.

Her arms felt numb. Her entire body was numb.

She hesitated before running down the stairs to answer the banging on the door.

Everything was moving too fast. It all felt so surreal. Her head was spinning uncontrollably as she watched the group of responders zap an electrical current through Dove's naked body.

The last thing she remembered was hearing someone yelling, "she's back!" before they whisked her away in the ambulance.

She slid herself against the wall until she was sitting on the hard floor and then she exhaled, this time for herself.

The house was filled with a certain solemn stillness.

An hour later, Raven was still sat in the same spot when a frantic Robyn came busting through the door.

"What's the emergency?" She asked as she glared at her sister who appeared lost.

"It's... Dove," she explained.

"What about Dove?" she questioned. "...and where is she?"

Her eyes searched the room but there were few traces of the chaos that had enveloped the room earlier.

There were no sirens, no naked bodies lying on the floor, no room full of emergency respondents.

"Dove tried to take her own life. She's going to be okay."

"What?" Robyn asked. "You're lying!" she yelled in disbelief. "Dove wouldn't do that to us... she wouldn't do that to herself... she has been so strong...why now?"

"Robyn..." Raven interrupted, her voice was wary as if she didn't have any strength left.

"She said she was fine," Robyn continued.

"Robyn!" Raven shouted, a visible vein popping up along her neck. "It's Quilt's birthday."

For a while, the two sat in silence.

"Dove showed us only what she wanted us to see, but think about it. She kept making excuses not to go back to work... a few weeks ago she donated an awful lot of stuff. You don't live here

Robyn... I do. Dove wore Quilt's clothes more than she did her own. At times she would seem fine, but she hasn't been the same Bird that we know."

Robyn felt she had failed her sister. How could she have ignored all the signs? She believed Dove had changed her name back to Williams because she was trying to forget Quilt, but she should've known that Dove would never abandon anything to do with Quilt. She planned this. The name change was to make it easier to for her mother to carry out her will.

She walked towards the bathroom. A sweet scent lingered around her nose. The tub was still filled with water and on the side, a glass-half full of wine.

Robyn sighed with relief, grateful that her sister had survived. She walked closer and reached for the glass, her shoes kicking a bottle on the ground. She picked up the pill bottle which was half empty. Her heart sinking as she read the inscription: *Take one tablet for pain.*

"Oh Dove!" she sobbed, "time is the only cure for heartache." The half full glass slipped from her hands, breaking as it crashed onto the floor into tiny pieces.

"You're cleaning that up!" Raven shouted from the other room, and they both began to laugh through their tears.

The sun hovered about the building, coating the sky with shades like cotton candy. Mrs. Williams sat watching her daughter sleep, she looked like an angel.

She couldn't say Dove was her favorite child. She had no favorite. But Dove was special. She remembered her first and her last pregnancy, they both had been uneventful, but with Dove, it was rough. Twice, she almost miscarried and as if that wasn't enough, the baby had decided to make her entrance a week early on the night of a full moon with an umbilical cord wrapped tightly around her neck.

Mrs. Williams had been told the baby wasn't breathing and she needed to be resuscitated. They gave her little chance of survival and were told that if she did, she would most likely end up with Cerebral Palsy.

But the baby defied all odds. She was her miracle baby. The child who would keep her in meetings with the principal at least once every month.

She smiled blissfully at the memory as she patted Dove's hand. She opened the photo diary in her cell phone and scrolled through pictures. Her eyes filled with water as she stared at one of Dove and Quilt. It was the night of their senior prom and Mrs. Williams remembered standing next to Dana and beaming at their children. Both had decided they were going to be rebellious and not follow the crowd to prom, *they weren't going to be sheep*, is what they said. They had hated the fact that their parents had forced them to go. She remembered taking an overwhelming number of pictures and Dove frowning in most of them calling them excessive and unnecessary.

Her daughter had very much look like a goddess in her embroidered bodice blue dress and Quilt was as handsome as ever in his black tuxedo. It was that night she knew her daughter was in love by the way she beamed at the boy next door. At seventeen, Dove was in love, though she wasn't quite sure Quilt was aware.

Quilt was fidgety and he hadn't been able to keep his eyes off her as she strolled down the stairs. He pulled out a blue corsage and gave it to Dove. This had been the very first time he had seen her all dressed up.

She watched until the two drove off in the rented limousine.

Later that night, her daughter came home bursting with joy and a paper ring on her finger. Quilt had finally kissed her and asked her to be his girl.

It saddened her that Quilt was now gone forever, but the memories were forever, and now she was thankful more than ever that she took those unnecessary pictures.

She scrolled through a few more before being interrupted by the doctor. Dr. Patel was a colleague of Mrs. Williams and also a friend.

"Elaine," she greeted her upon walking through the door.

"Hello Reena."

The two embraced for a quick second.

Dove eyes flickered as she awakened from her sleep. The voices becoming more recognizable. It felt like she had been sleeping for days. The last thing she remembered was talking to her mother about scrambled eggs and now it appeared the sun was making its decent. She glanced at the sky.

Mom is still here, she thought.

"Hello Dove," the doctor smiled upon noticing she was awake.

"Hey honey," Mrs. Williams said. Her eyes were still filled with concern for her. After all, she was a psychiatrist and she knew the battle with severe depression was never quick nor easy.

"Elaine, do you mind giving me a few minutes alone with Dove?" the doctor asked.

Mrs. Williams's mouth tightened as if the request was highly unreasonable.

"It's okay Dr. Patel," Dove said interrupting her mother's incoming rebuttal.

"Very well then," she said. "From a psychiatric standpoint, I have recommended your discharge for tomorrow. However, I would like to recommend that you take the prescription that I have placed in the chart."

Dr. Patel started going into great details about the medication, but Dove's mind had drifted away. All she could think about was Quilt being in the sky as she gazed at the clouds.

"Isn't that dosage a bit excessive?" Mrs. Williams questioned, sounding a bit overbearing.

Dr. Patel's eyes narrowed, shooting a disapproving look at her friend before turning back to Dove.

"Any questions Dove?" She placed emphasis on Dove's name.

Dove shook her head.

"Okay!" She tucked the pad and pen inside of her jacket. "You know how to reach me if something comes up." She turned towards the door.

"Elaine," she said, "can I speak with you in the hall?"

She watched the two ladies walk into the hallway. Dove pretended as if she couldn't overhear everything they were discussing about her. She had lost all care and she repeated every word as mockery inside her head: "Dove is suffering from depression which could worsen. She needs continued treatment and support."

"Dove will be fine," she heard her mother say.

"Elaine you are thinking like a mother and not a doctor. You of all people should know there are some great facilities for depression and anxiety. Please consider it."

Wait! She thought. *Treatment center?*

Now she cared, because all she wanted to do was to be at home, in her bed, where the smell of Quilt still lingered.

She had spent three long days in the hospital and she was ready to go home.

Mrs. Williams walked back into the room.

"I can't wait to go home tomorrow," Dove smiled at her. She pretended not to notice her reaction, the one that said, *Dove, you're not going home.*

CHAPTER TWELVE

The Lamp Shade

"It's a beautiful day out!" Dove's mother pulled the curtains from the awning windows. She pushed the windows outward and allowed the air to flow in. At the top of her lungs, she proudly hummed the words to Amazing Grace.

Dove laid in bed, the white cotton sheets pulled high above her head. She could not decide if her mom was crazy or just plain rude. Maybe she was both. Here she was... at seven in the morning, interrupting her sleep.

Dove was still angry at her mother's ultimatum to seek treatment at this isolated place. She had agreed to a week, yet it was nine days later, and she wasn't home.

"Mom!" she yelled from under the covers. "Can you please not do that!" Her words were cold; she had meant to sound rude.

Mrs. Williams continued as if she hadn't heard her.

"The coordinator mentioned a boating activity today. I think we should go," she sounded excited.

"Yes... lets!" Dove said with pure sarcasm. "Maybe I'll get lucky and drown."

Mrs. Williams dropped the clothes she was folding. Her feet stomped as she marched over to the bed. With a strong force, she whipped the covers from Dove's head.

She stared at her with eyes wide and intense. "Watch your mouth young lady." She spoke firmly. "I don't think you get it. You isolate yourself at home, you lock yourself up in this room.

You're not home because you are not making any progress. You have an illness and the cure is not suicide, Dove. The answer is living."

Dove sat up in the bed. "I don't belong here. This place is for the crazies and..."

"...people like you!" Mrs. Williams shouted. "It's for people like you who need help with depression."

"But I didn't ask for help. I wanted to be with my husband so what's wrong with that!"

"What's wrong with that you ask?" Mrs. Williams was now extremely angry. "The answer is you my dear, was willing to put others in the very same pain you are now trying to escape. So, you ask yourself, what's wrong with that!?"

Mrs. Williams continued "I know this pain seems unbearable, but there are people who are fighting daily to overcome adversity. A few weeks ago, I had to inject a patient with a drug called Memaxonal to suppress her childhood memories of sexual abuse." She spoke with passion in her voice. "It was her will to survive that has kept her going for all these years. Her medication, much like your therapy, is to help you persevere.

Dove got up from the bed and walked over to the window. Leaning against the windowsill as if she desperately needed to inhale fresh air.

"Why don't you just come out and say it then? You think I'm a coward, you think I'm selfish... and... and... you look at me as if you are ashamed," she spat, her voice breaking with her words.

Mrs. Williams rose from the bed. Her thumb wiped away the water that had gathered on her daughter's cheek. "I'm not ashamed of you. You are one of the strongest people I have ever known and now, your strength is just a tad bit broken, but there's redemption for all of us." She smiled as she pushed back the strands from her face to kiss her forehead. "You are my life and I will do whatever it takes to save you."

"I'm sorry mom," she cried. "I've tried to be strong but next to dad, losing Quilt was the greatest pain I've ever known. Everyone tells me time is going to heal but every day the wound gets deeper and deeper and now it's just a flesh-eating infection. No one told me it would stink this badly!" she spewed, "what started as subtle little white lies, it's just a bad day and now it's a hundred different shades of blue that scream at me. Depression shouts that things will never get better... that somehow this is all my fault, that there's no hope. I needed the silence!"

"Baby, it does get better. I promise!"

She wanted to believe her but Dove just couldn't see herself in this world being happy without Quilt. It was just too far-fetched. Still she nodded, at least she still held a bit of hope that her mother was right.

Mrs. Williams spoke to her daughter for a while. She told her of all the things she had learned from pain. She wanted Dove to know that pain was an inevitable consequence of life and though pain can be incapacitating, it is necessary for growth.

"Water is therapy. Get dressed. I think this boat trip will be good for you," Mrs. Williams said sternly and then she was out the door.

The lake glistened with the light from the sun. Like metal, it shined, emitting flashes of silver on the surface of the water. It was as if magic had been cast upon the lake. The smell of pine swept the air with the gentle blow of the wind and softly ruffled the trees along the shore. It was tranquility at its best. Dove tilted her head back, closed her eyes and inhaled deeply. She felt a touch tracing along the nape of her neck. And though she knew it was the wind, she still imagined it was Quilt running his fingers down her golden skin. *Gosh, I miss you*, she thought.

She smiled feeling the sun kissing her skin, and she knew he had answered. He missed her too. An unexplainable feeling of warmth flowed inside her. She sniffed her white cotton shirt which now smelled of a hint citrus mixed with leather.

"What sorcery is this?" she questioned, a smile still lingered around her lips. She opened her eyes to find her mother eyes fixated on her, deep creases burrowed on her forehead.

"Just enjoying nature," Dove said in response to her mother's unspoken questions.

"I told you this is therapy," her mother smiled feeling a bit pleased with herself.

"Mom, if I tell you something could you promise to keep an open mind and put away your psychiatrist hat?"

Mrs. Williams lied. She wished she could tell her daughter the truth, that her work had always directed her to better understand people and though she tried not to do it in her personal life, her daughter was that exception... at least for now. Dove needed help and since she was a psychiatrist and not a psychic, she would have to get her daughter to be open. "Yes," she lied. She was analyzing everything to help her the best way she could.

"Do you believe in reincarnation?"

"I try to keep an open mind but what about you Dove... what do you believe?"

"I didn't, but since Quilt passed he has been visiting me." She continued, despite her mother's blank stare. "He comes to me as birds," she laughed, "isn't that just like Quilt? The first night he came as a Dove but mostly as a Northern Cardinal." She paused, and a tiny smile crept across her face. "He always said it was his favorite bird." She giggled. "One day there was a crane in the yard. It was the weirdest thing, but I would recognize Quilt's eyes anywhere. You're quiet... do you think I'm crazy?" Dove asked.

"The concept of soul is such an intrinsic part of many religions. I've met a great deal of people who believe that when a person passes, the soul somehow survives and returns to this world to fulfill a purpose. Reena for one, believes that the soul comes back temporarily as an animal. She said it is incarnated four times, with each incarnation becoming more powerful until it is human."

"So, does that mean you believe?" Dove asked.

"What I believe is that the mind is much more powerful than any drug and sometimes the things we create in our mind can become our reality. So yes Dove, I do believe you have seen Quilt." Mrs. Williams smiled, not indicating the uneasiness that was brewing inside of her. It wasn't that Dove was seeing her dead husband in the form of birds, but her concern that she may never truly move on to accept that Quilt was gone forever. And for a minute she abandoned all concern as she eyed Dove bubbling with laughter when a group of spotted trout leaped out of the water, exhibiting their gift of vertical flight as the boat frolicked along the waters. She understood what Dove needed and it was clear that her daughter needed her.

"Honey, why don't you spend a few days at the house with me instead of in that big house?" Mrs. Williams asked, "It would be great for you and Raven."

"But mom..." she protested.

"You would be able to get out of this place a few days early," she bribed.

Dove gave it some serious thought before agreeing. Anything was better than being in an unfamiliar place and sharing her feelings with complete strangers.

* * *

"Where do you think you're going?" Mrs. Williams said to Raven.

Raven grabbed her car keys from the kitchen counter. "I'm meeting Kevin for dinner remember?"

It was a gorgeous Friday evening and she certainly didn't plan on babysitting for another night. She had done so for the past three weeks and frankly, she was tired of it. Her boyfriend and social life had been neglected long enough and she promised herself that tonight she would have some fun. Her mother had convinced Dove to stay for a couple of days, now it was going on three weeks. Someone had to always be home, keeping an eye on her as if Dove was a child.

Robyn had been as helpful as she could be, but she had a family of her own to take care of. Much of the responsibility had fallen on Raven much like when she had moved in with Dove after Quilt's death.

"Raye, I had specifically told you about the function I had tonight. You mentioned you didn't have plans," Mrs. Williams said, sounding frustrated.

"Mom, things changed."

".... yes, and they can change again," her mother replied before snatching the keys from her hand.

She threw the keys back on the counter and walked into the living room.

Raven followed, her feet heavy as if a sasquatch was hitting the floor. "I don't see why we can't both go out? She's fine!" she said pointing towards the stairs.

Mrs. Williams faced her daughter. Her eyes narrowed with pupils much darker than Raven could remember. Every line on her face seemed more pronounced and, in that moment, Raven knew she wouldn't be going out. Not this Friday night.

"Must I explain the five stages of grief to you again?" Mrs. Williams asked through clenched teeth. She held up her hand exposing the palm of her hand as she counted each stage. "Your sister is stuck at depression. She doesn't need to be alone."

"Fine!" Raven shouted and threw her purse on the couch. "This will be my last night in this house. I'm moving in with Kevin," she yelled on her way upstairs.

There was a worm moon visible in the east of the sky. Dove sat quietly enjoying the moonrise. How many times she had climb this balcony after missing her curfew? Her balcony had allowed her to see the moon clear the horizon in the evenings. The view was remarkable, and she doubted any cloud would dare ruin it.

Tonight, it reminded her of the one time her father took her camping. She could still hear the crickets and the melodies of spring creepers calling their mates. The sulfurous smell of the pond was enough to make her never attempt camping again. Though something about that experience had made her feel closer to her father, as if that was even possible. Now she had lost the two people that she was the closest to in the world.

A creak came from the door to her room. She turned her head towards the sound of the footsteps.

"Hey," Raven spoke softly. She tucked her hands into the pockets of her blue jeans.

"Hi," Dove said, and she placed her lips on the warm cup in her hands.

"I made sandwiches," Raven said enthusiastically "...turkey club – your favorite."

"Thanks Raye, but I'm not really hungry."

"What about some punch? Heavily spiked, but don't tell mom," she joked.

Dove forced a tight-lipped smile and then turned her head towards the moon.

"I'm through trying," Raven said.

"I know you think that I'm a burden Raye!" Dove shouted in her direction.

An angry Raven found her way back onto the balcony. She had always allowed Dove to wallow in her grief, but not today. Today she hit a wall and she wanted her to know of the burden she had placed on the family. The pain she had put her and Robyn through... and her mother... her own mother was so fearful that she would harm herself again that she was negating the fact that she had two other children who had lives of their own.

"No Dove, I don't think you're a burden. I think you are selfish," she shouted. "What you have asked of us is to watch you kill yourself, and what you continue to ask of us is to watch you drown in despair. We're all sick of it!" Raven continued, grabbing the opportunity to lash out at Dove's silence. "Quilt is gone but he wouldn't want you to live this way."

"Quilt is not gone!" Dove fired back angrily. "He is still here... even if he is a bird, he's still here!"

"A bird?" Raven questioned. She was confused or maybe she just misunderstood. "Do you hear yourself?" she laughed mockingly. Raven threw her hands up in the air, she had now heard it all, "you're not a burden Dove, maybe you're just crazy."

Dove's eyes grew red. Inside she was boiling. Her hands were balled up in a fist and her breathing erratic. How dare Raye make a mockery of Quilt. "I think it's time for you to leave," she warned through clenched teeth.

Raven eyed her sister's fist. She knew when to walk away from an argument with Dove. She had learned from previous fights. "Okay," she said, "Robyn is coming over. I'm leaving."

Dove knew her family loved her, but it was extremely hard for her to see herself other than a burden. She felt helpless. The greatest love she had ever known was gone. How does a person move on from that? She didn't know how, and no one had the answers. She felt so lost, so helpless. There was a gaping hole that she just couldn't seem to fill. The one piece of light she had held onto was that Quilt had somehow returned to comfort her but what if Raye was right? What if she really was just crazy?

She wanted her mind to stop thinking. She begged her heart to stop aching. Her insides were in turmoil. She wanted it to end.

Raven answered the continuous ring at the door and an impatient Robyn strutted through the door. "Took you long enough!" she snarled at Raven.

"Well hello to you too." Raven said. "Sorry Raye but I've been outside for what feels like forever." She stopped and examined the leaky mascara around her baby sister's eyes. "What's wrong?" she asked. It was starting to feel like déjà vu.

Raven sniffled, "I just got in an argument with Dove and I probably shouldn't have said anything, but I told her we were all sick of her moods."

"Raye!" Robyn gasped, "no!"

Raven nodded.

"There's no timestamp on grief... I can't imagine losing..."

A very loud thump interrupted her words.

"Dove!" Raven uttered, a fearful look crossed her face, and both darted up the stairs.

In the corner of the room, a light flickered from a fallen lamp. A wooden chair rested on the floor, next to it was the missing piece of its broken leg. Dove's body laid still, above her hung a cord tied around the ceiling fan.

"Dove!" they screamed simultaneously, fear gripping both.

Specks of blood splashed on the wall and saturated the cream-colored carpet where her head rested.

Robyn panicked, vigorously shaking her sister's shoulders.

"Dove!" she shouted.

Dove moaned and a sigh of relief escaped her sister's lips.

"It's Robyn... can you open your eyes?"

"Quilt," Dove whispered continuously.

They heard the front door open.

"Mom?" Raven called, her voice was filled with uncertainty.

"Raye?" she answered in a worrisome voice.

Mrs. Williams hurried up the stairs, surveying the room on entrance... a broken chair, a rope, blood. She gasped aloud, and her bag fell to the floor.

Dove moaned again, and Mrs. Williams hurried to her side, pushing aside the chair. "The chair broke," she smiled. Never had she been so happy to have a broken piece of furniture. "Raye get me a couple of wet washcloths and my medical bag. Robyn help me place her on the bed."

Raven hurried back, her hands shaky as she handed her mother the cloths.

Mrs. Williams cleaned the laceration on the back of Dove's head before dressing the wound.

"Quilt... Quilt, I won't give up until I find you," Dove repeated several times.

Mrs. Williams knew in her heart, this would not be her daughter's last attempt. They all felt it. Dove was the most obstinate human being they all knew. She would keep trying... this wasn't the end.

"Shh," Mrs. Williams silenced her daughter. She gently stroked her face until she heard snoring from Dove's mouth.

"What now?" A tearful Raven asked.

"She's going to be fine," Mrs. Williams said.

"But mom you heard her, she won't stop," Robyn interjected.

"I said she will be fine," she re-iterated.

"I have to disagree. Dove needs some serious help. She needs more than just a week or two at some fancy facility or... we will lose her forever."

Mrs. Williams had a very long experience in psychiatry. She knew that depression was a battle. She was aware of the stigma. She had treated many and was very much aware of the high rate for relapse. What she was also aware of was the disparity in the mental health system. She was not going to allow her precious daughter to end up between the cracks of such a system. Not when she was a trained psychiatrist who was more than capable of giving her child the best care at home.

"I will do what is best for my child... right here at home." She glared at her daughters and her words were filled with disappointment. "Besides... I begged you two to look after your sister and here she is laying in a pool of blood. That's the proof

I need that I'm the only one that cares enough to save her." Her words were sharp, and Raven felt herself bleed, especially since she had given up so much to help with Dove.

"Well I think you're ashamed… ashamed of what people will say… a highly respected psychiatrist with a certifiable crazy child. That's the real reason you want to keep this controlled!" Raven spat with the intention of wounding her mother, "how would your ego survive?"

Mrs. Williams opened her mouth widely and then she closed it as if she had decided to abandon her initial response. "I know what you're doing, and my decision still stands. I will take care of my daughter."

"…and how do we do that? Do we continue watching over her for the rest of our lives? Because frankly we haven't done a good job at it!" Robyn cried.

"Memaxonal," Mrs. Williams spoke softly.

Raven's mouth opened. She could not believe what she was hearing. She blinked several times, hoping to see an inkling of humor on her mother's face.

"You're joking right?"

"No. We must make her forget. If Dove is going to survive then we have to wipe out all memories of Quilt and anything linking him to her."

Robyn sat quietly.

"Robyn please say something, tell mom that this is not right. Those are Dove's memories. It's not right to take them from her!" Raven cried.

Mrs. Williams began to cry. "Those memories are going to kill your sister. Now it's either him or her!" she shouted.

"I'm with mom Raye," Robyn spoke, "I just can't handle another loss."

Raven rubbed her temple. She could feel the pressure building in her head. "That's something we shouldn't get to decide. Would you want your memories erased if that was Dennis?"

Robyn hesitated before answering. Her words were careful as she spoke. "If I knew it would kill me then yes, I would want to forget."

Mrs. Williams placed her hands on Raven's shoulders. She desperately wanted her to understand. "We will tell everyone she was in an accident... that she doesn't remember. We can request that they don't bring certain memories up because it can harm her."

"Raye, it would be a temporary solution...maybe for a few months." Robyn added.

"Well, sounds like you two have it all figured out. I can't be a part of this." Raven said before storming out the room.

The lamp flickered a few more time before going completely out.

Robyn reached towards the light switch on the wall.

"No," Mrs. Williams told her, "leave her in the dark."

CHAPTER THIRTEEN

Rebirth

Dove cautiously removed the chicken from the oven. It was almost a month since she had moved back into her home and exactly one week since she returned from a trip with Raven. Mexico had been lovely but now she was ready to put the pieces of her life together. A life she felt had been neglected. Especially her home. She bought new curtains. She rearranged her furniture and she had finally decided to make use of her kitchen again.

She knew there were places, people and memories missing. Her mother had explained to her all about her car accident. The accident she could not remember but had somehow robbed her of sacred things.

Unbeknownst to her, her family had swept the house clean of any traces of Quilt, yet his essence remained. After all, the man had pretty much designed the house.

Once again, Raven had moved in with Dove. A part of her still resented her mother for the choice she had made, although Raven had come to see some good in her decision. Dove was smiling again, she was venturing out, but Raven did notice she was not completely the same person. The new Dove was far less self-destructive. She was thinking before she spoke, and hated parties, instead preferring to stay home and lose herself in music. One thing that had not changed though... she hated the smell of coffee.

Dove placed the pan on the back of the stove. She was very pleased with the way her dish came out. Now she just needed to get started on her sides. She should've started a while ago, but she had been distracted by something on the television; a woman had been murdered in a nearby town.

She added some flour then slowly added milk, briskly whisking with each additional ingredient.

The doorbell rang a few times. She let it ring a few more before she abandoned her cooking. She wasn't expecting anyone. Dove untied the strings to her apron, tossing it on the kitchen counter.

She pulled the door open to view the tall figure standing before her. He looked like he had been dipped in bronze and his hair was the color of night.

She was a bit flustered by his extraordinary good looks. *He had to know he was beautiful... he had to,* Dove thought as she tried not to stare directly into his eyes.

"Hi, I'm Ryan. I live a few houses down the street," he smiled lazily as he pointed to his house.

The wind sent a whiff of his scent straight to her nostrils and it hit her like a batter hit a pitch.

She caught it, the scent, it was familiar... earthy, sandalwood. Perhaps it was leather? And it made parts of her tingle.

"Dove," she replied as she shook his hand. She was surprised by the softness for someone so masculine.

"Did the Westbrooks move out?" she asked, eyeing the taupe house down the street. She had always hated that house. Just something about it was very creepy. The giant oak tree in the front yard only added to the mystery.

"No, I'm their nephew. My uncle is ill so I'm staying with them awhile to help out."

"Oh, you're a transplant!" she teased.

"A transplant?"

"You know... someone who has moved in from a different state."

He laughed, "Oh, Seattle!"

She remembers stopping in Seattle for a flight layover. From what she remembered it was cold and rained a lot.

"Home of the most beautiful grey skies," she smiled.

He chuckled revealing a smile that seemed genuinely sweet. The alignment of his teeth was pure perfection.

"So how may I help you Ryan?" she asked after an awkward moment of silence.

"Sorry, guess I was trying to forget giving you the bad news."

Dove searched his face for answers, she folded her arms and tapped her fingers against her biceps. Her eyebrows hit each other like a head on car crash, while her eyes remained fixated on his mouth.

She hated bad news.

"If that's your car in front of your house... then I'm here to apologize and to let you know that I will cover the damages to your passenger door."

Dove tried to see the damages, but the green velvet boxwood in the front of the yard blocked her view.

"Yes, what happened?" she asked. The news was not as bad as she had been anticipating.

"Let me just say that I will also cover your rental during the repair." He cleared his throat. "So out of nowhere a stupid bird flew right in front of me. I swerved and hit your car. But on the bright side... the bird survived," he added with a touch of humor.

"A bird?" she asked.

"Yeah. Sounds crazy doesn't it? It had a beautiful red shade, like fire. I'm not familiar with those species in Seattle."

"Sounds like a cardinal," said Dove, "there's one that is always by my window and I agree, they're beautiful."

He smiled at her and then for a moment, his eyes followed behind her, concern wiping the smile from his face. "There's smoke coming from that room."

She turned quickly in a panic, eyeing the cloud of grey smoke coming from the kitchen. Dove had completely forgotten about the stove and she ran towards the room. The handsome stranger quickly followed behind her.

The smell of charred milk enveloped the room and the flames swayed joyously as they devoured the apron on the counter.

"Stand back!" Ryan ordered, snatching the small extinguisher mounted on the wall. He doused the stove with the white powdery mixture, sweeping from left to right until the flames were completely gone.

"Well dinner is ruined," she joked.

Ryan seemed less amused. He pushed the window to the kitchen open, allowing fresh air to flow into the kitchen.

"Fires aren't amusing Dove," he said sternly. His face reminding her of her father's when he had found out she had skipped school and went joyriding. She remembered that she had been scolded at fifteen and it made her feel as if she was an imbecile as she felt the same right now.

"Do you replace the batteries in your smoke detector?" he asked while gazing at the ceiling.

"I meant to, but I just keep forgetting," she replied softly as if she was afraid the answer might bring about punishment.

He examined the kitchen some more, as if he was trying to find something else that was wrong.

"What's all this commotion down here?" Raven walked in the kitchen, sweeping her feet. She rubbed her eyes while yawning as if she hadn't just gotten at least nine hours of sleep. She had partied all night and slept most of the day away.

"Just a little burnt pot and smoke," Ryan explained.

"Well that pretty much sums up Dove's cooking," she said. She grabbed an apple from the island and took a loud bite into the piece of fruit. "...I'm sorry and who are you?" she asked as if she had just realized there was a stranger in the room.

"Ryan," he said, the frown disappearing from his face. "Your neighbor from down the street."

"Well Ryan, our neighbor from down the street. I'm Dove's sister, Raven," she said before eagerly taking another bite.

"So, you both have names of birds?" His lips curled upward.

"Wow, handsome and smart. Dove don't let this one go," Raven said with a hint of sarcasm.

"Raye!" Dove said and then she apologized for her sister's tone.

Raven mimicked her sister's words.

Ryan, with pure amusement, tilted his head back and laughed.

"Am I missing something?" Dove asked upon noticing Raven was trying hard to suppress her laughter. She felt left out of whatever amusement the two had seemed to share.

Neither answered.

"Okay, well it was nice meeting you Ryan. Now excuse me, as you can see I'll will have to go fetch dinner. Raye can you show our neighbor the way out?" Dove was visibly annoyed. The man had just scolded her for a mistake, yet here he was being Mr. Delightful with Raye.

He reached for her arm as he walked towards the door. A small amount of electricity jolted through her body – small enough that she hoped no one else noticed.

"Dove," he said softly, hypnotizing her with his good looks. "Would it be okay if I took you out to eat? I feel bad for everything I've caused today."

"It's really not your fault. Please, Ryan, don't blame yourself."

"Please let me buy you dinner," he insisted.

Dove found the notion to be very sweet but although he was charming, she hardly knew the man. For all she knew he could be the axe murderer she'd heard about on the news.

"Thank you, Ryan, but I'm a little tired and pizza and a movie is starting to look real appealing right about now," she smiled.

Raven walked towards them. "What?" she said rolling her eyes, "we had pizza two nights ago. Ryan the dinner you ruined was also mine, so we will see you in an hour. Make it an hour and a half because Dove takes forever to get dressed."

He smiled and looked at his watch. "Great, I'll be here at seven." He seemed very pleased.

Raven knew her sister was oblivious when someone of the opposite sex liked her. She had witnessed it firsthand on their recent vacation to Mexico. It pleased her that she possessed the one thing that Dove was terrible at – the art of flirting. She just didn't seem to be very good at it, and why would she? Quilt had been her one and only since childhood. For her no one else had even existed.

Raven smiled, feeling quite pleased with herself. She had felt a certain projection for a desire to get to know the stranger.

* * *

The atmosphere in Tuscany was very relaxed, the small restaurant was both family oriented and romantic. The candles on the table complemented the warm orange colors on the wall. Inside smelled of freshly baked bread and herbs mixed with the rich aroma of roasted garlic. Their table was situated in the center of the room. Above, a chandelier shined on the wooden beams. It dripped with diamonds and coatings of gold.

Dove had to admit that this was much better than sitting at home eating pizza. She bopped her head to the tempo of the background music as she skimmed through the menu. Raven smiled each time she caught Ryan stealing a couple of glances at her sister. What she also noticed was the very thirsty group of ladies that drooled every time they looked his way. Raven knew she had to work fast to find out if he was a suitable match for her sister, but Dove was slightly embarrassed by the way Raven drilled their neighbor.

How old was he? Twenty-eight.

Did he have any kids? No

Did he have siblings? One brother; one sister.

She had tried to stop her a few times, but he insisted it was okay.

If she hadn't known that Raye was naturally filled with curiosity, then she would've thought her sister was trying to play matchmaker.

Ryan's cellphone rang, and he excused himself from the table to accept the call.

"I think he likes you!" Raven whispered.

"You're acting pushy," she whispered back at her.

She took a sip of her water as she eyed Ryan making his way back to the table.

"Call from your girlfriend?" Raven asked coyly.

Dove gasped, almost choking between sips of water. Her cheeks felt as if they were on fire.

"Raye!"

He laughed, once again finding Raven amusing although his eyes were fixated on Dove. He seemed to enjoy her expression and the way she squirmed every time the younger sister said something outrageous.

"No Raye," he grinned, "I don't have a girlfriend. Just a call from my aunt. I don't have many friends here, she was worried."

"Excellent!" Raven grinned.

"If you ask any more questions, I'm will start to think you are interested in me," he smirked.

Raven swallowed the bite of bread in her mouth "Yes, but not for me. I'm taken so eat your heart out. Dove is the single one," and she grinned from ear to ear. Her laugh was sinister, and she stuffed another bite in her mouth.

Dove's cheeks had escaped Miami and somehow ended up in the Sahara Desert. How badly she wanted to crawl under the table.

He was amused, loving the way her face betrayed her every emotion.

She contemplated making a dash for the door, but the waiter interrupted with their meals.

* * *

"How's your dinner?" Ryan asked after a period of silence.

"Wonderful," Dove replied without making eye contact.

Ryan apologized for his behavior earlier. He explained that he was a firefighter and had seen too many lives ruined from not having a simple smoke detector. She listened as he revealed that he had also lost his father that way. There was such sincerity in him and she found a kindness in his soul. Somewhere under that muscular exterior was something very soft.

The conversation flowed smoothly. The loss of a parent resonated with Dove, for it was a tragedy to which she could relate.

She was surprised to find the many other things that they had in common: Both were the middle child, both shared a love for black and white movies and both had grown up with parents who were Baptist.

Meanwhile, a quiet Raven pretended to be busy texting but taking credit for how perfectly her plan was going.

"More wine?" he asked.

Dove declined. She had drunk a little too much and was starting to feel sleepy. She also ate a lot, leaving very little on her plate.

"You've been awfully quiet," Dove said to Raven.

"Sorry, Kevin is in a texting mood tonight," she lied.

Ryan smiled, "It sounds like Kevin is a man in love."

"What about you Ryan, have you ever been in love?" Raven asked.

"Maybe once or twice," he answered. "...and you Dove, have you ever been in love?"

Raven's heartbeat escalated, and she swallowed forcefully to rid the lump that had climbed in her throat.

"Not sure," Dove answered innocently.

Ryan's brows furrowed. It didn't quite make sense to him, and he didn't believe it was an honest answer.

"I believe there's no in between with something as strong as love. It's either you have or have not. So, Dove, have you ever been in love?" he asked again.

Let it go! Raven screamed inside her head.

She watched as his lips began to form another set of words.

"Well," she said before he could speak, "Dove was in an accident that affected some memory, so she really can't be sure."

"Thanks Raven, next time say it louder for the people in the back." Dove felt uncomfortable. It wasn't something she would have ever revealed to a stranger.

"Sorry," Raven apologized. She knew that she was wrong for sharing but she had panicked and just needed Ryan to drop the issue.

"To answer your question, I will say no, I've never been in love. I don't think my memory would have let me forget something as beautiful as being in love," Dove said.

Raven felt a sharp pain on the inside. Her mind began to race. She thought about Quilt. Maybe he was twisting her heart? It ached, more than it had before. Or maybe it was just her guilt. Secrets had never sat well with her. She felt bad for Dove... and Ryan. Poor Ryan. It was obvious he liked her. If only he knew the depth of love Dove had experienced... he wouldn't stand a chance if she had her memory.

How dare her mother play with faith like this. She felt sick to her stomach.

"Dove..." she said, interrupting a string of laughter between the two. "I'm not feeling well, can we go?"

"Oh Raye, you don't look well. Was it something you ate?"

Ryan signaled for the waiter while the ladies excused themselves to the bathroom. Ryan didn't want the night to end. It had been a while since he had enjoyed himself around the opposite sex. He watched as the ladies made their way back to the table, his eyes focused on one.

Why would a woman like her be single? he thought. *She has never been in love, but I bet she has broken many hearts, she seems like the type. The type that would get a man so wrapped up in his feelings then leave because of her fear of commitment.*

"How are you feeling?" he asked Raven.

She was about to answer when she heard a song playing in the background. *Seriously!?* She wanted to scream at the universe, *Her wedding song?*

Dove's eyes lit up. She struggled as she tried to figure out the significance of the song that had triggered a flash of her holding someone's hand. It had also touched her soul very deeply for some reason.

"This song. I know this song," she said softly, closing her eyes.

"Unchained Melody," Ryan smiled.

"Yes," she beamed for a moment which was interrupted when she noticed the greenish glow that had crept into her sister's skin. "Raye, you look like death. Let's get you home."

* * *

It was almost eleven a.m. and Dove had slept much later than she had intended. Sundays were for curling up to a good book on the couch anyways. She was pretty sure that's how she would be spending the day.

She checked in on Raven, but it seems that she had already been gone for the day. Her thoughts drifted back to the spectacular time she had with Ryan last night. His smile was like lightning, both beautiful and dangerous – for some reason she remembered it the most.

She hit the switch to the bathroom. An instant ache appeared at the back of her head. It felt like someone was trapped and knocking on a door, begging to get out. It had happened a few times. A distant memory of a figure that just never seemed to surface.

Dove splashed some water on her skin and began to wash her face. She liked what she saw in the mirror, eyes clear, skin glowing. A smile lingered around her lips.

"You're smitten," she said out loud, then quickly brushed it off. "Smitten with the love of tea," she said dismissing her thoughts, before heading downstairs.

She searched the cabinets and it seemed she was out of tea. She was also out of hot chocolate and it appeared she was out of many other things. She made a list. Today she would spend the day grocery shopping.

After a long hot shower, she got dressed and then sent a text to her baby sister.

Dove: Hey Raye, how are you feeling?

Raye: Much better.

Dove: Are you with Kevin?

Raye: Yes.

Dove: What do you want for dinner?

Raye: Spending the night at Kevin's.

Dove: Great! Do you need anything from the market?

Before she could read Raye's next response, the doorbell rang.

It was Ryan, donned in a pair of grey sweats, a blue t-shirt and sneakers. There were beads of sweat on his forehead. She backed away from the peep hole and straightened her hair once, then again.

"Hi," she smiled broadly as she opened the door.

"Hello."

"Where are we running to?" she asked, addressing his choice of outfit.

"Fiji," he said playfully.

She imagined the playfulness of a tiger but dangerous enough to kill you in just one swipe.

"May I come in?"

"Yes, I'm sorry." She stepped aside allowing him to enter.

He revealed something in his hand. "With your permission, I wanted to change the batteries in your smoke detectors."

"That's very thoughtful of you. Thank you, Ryan," she said.

He watched her lips formed a smile. On more than one occasion he found himself thinking how great it would be to kiss them.

They moved towards the kitchen. Ryan retrieved the ladder he had noticed in the backyard. Dove watched as he climbed upwards. She got flustered with all the thoughts running through her head.

"Raye? Dove?" the voice called from the living room. "Seriously, you guys left the door open. I swear you all are just one step away from ending up on the ten o'clock news," Robyn complained all the way into the kitchen.

"Hey Robyn," Dove greeted.

She removed her sunglasses, her eyes meeting with the stranger's.

"Sorry, I didn't realize my sister had company," she apologized.

"Robyn Ryan... Ryan Robyn," Dove said abruptly.

"A proper introduction would be nice," she glowered at her sister before kissing her on the cheek.

Ryan climbed down. "Hi, I'm Ryan and it's very nice to meet you Robyn," he smiled politely.

She shook his hand firmly and in less than a minute Ryan had summed up Robyn. She was competitive, an overachiever, possibly a control freak.

"Did mom send you to check on us again?"

"As if I need a reason to stop by to see my sisters," she shook her head, "I'm having dinner at my house next Sunday. Consider it a personal invite. Pass the message on to Raye."

"Will do but the phone still works for calls and texts, Robyn," Dove replied. She knew Robyn was doing her mother's dirty work by frequently spying on her. She also knew to expect a call later from her mother about the man in her house.

"Dove can I have a word with you?" Robyn asked.

She didn't wait on Dove's response and she pulled her towards the living room. "Who is this guy?"

"A neighbor," Dove replied.

"A neighbor?" she questioned. "I've never met this neighbor. I need to leave but I can stay if you need me to?"

"He's safe Robyn."

"Well here," she reached into her purse, "here's my Taser, just in case."

Ryan chuckled to himself, overhearing the conversation. Robyn wasn't a very good whisperer.

"Robyn put that away!" Dove said, a bewildered look crossing her face.

"If you insist," she said. She hugged her sister goodbye and urged her to call if she needed anything.

Dove watched from the kitchen window as Ryan placed the ladder in the backyard. She was practically drooling at the way his sweats clung to his body. Part of her wished he would ask her out again but maybe he didn't have as much of a good time than she had hoped. She reminded herself not to seem too eager, she didn't want to appear desperate.

He turned around, meeting her gaze and she realized it was too late to look away. He had pretty much caught her being a stalker.

He smiled.

She waved, then hung her head, feeling a bit of embarrassment.

"Thanks for replacing the batteries," she said as he walked in. She cleared the knot in the back of her throat.

"That reminds me. If it's okay, my mechanic can pick up your car at two today and have it back to you by Wednesday. He owes me," he smiled.

"Oh...my car." She had completely forgotten about the damage. "Yeah...that should be fine."

"What's wrong?" he asked. "We can go to any mechanic you choose. It's just that they might take a bit longer."

She rubbed her forehead. "No, it's not that... it's just that I was about to go grocery shopping and I completely forgot about the accident."

"I can take you."

She shook her head. "No, you have to be in Fiji."

He laughed, enjoying her sense of humor.

"Besides, you've met Robyn, she would love to take me, so she can grill me some more."

"Dove," he said firmly, lifting her chin, "I'm taking you."

She suddenly became very flustered as she imagined a sexual undertone in his response.

"Okay," she agreed, and she took a step back to grab the door keys.

* * *

The Farmer's market was usually stuffed with consumers and vendors and it would only take a slight turn to bump into someone. People would climb on each other liked crabs in a bucket. But not today. She was expecting the parking lot to be hell on wheels with drivers flying into spaces to grab an empty spot, but the chaos and noises close to the level of a construction site had been replaced with only a few chatters. Dove thought about shopping on Sundays from now on.

Ryan pushed the cart as she filled it with things from her list. He laughed quietly as he noticed some of the things that were written: Red wine, white wine and batteries for the smoke detectors. The last one had a line through it since it had already been replaced.

"There's something else I should've told you about why I became a firefighter," he said as they walked towards the produce section, "I was also in that fire that killed my father. I was around nine and my siblings and I barely made it out ourselves."

She stopped for a moment. "Oh, Ryan... I'm so sorry." Her heart ached for the little boy and the man standing in front of her. For the horror of witnessing a tragedy at such young age. Her eyes began to tear.

"Dove, it's okay," he smiled. "We all did well for ourselves. Our mother abandoned us soon after the incident, I think it was just too much for her to deal with emotionally, but the Westbrooks took us in and made sure we had the best of everything. That's why I'm here – to make sure they are taken care of." He smiled, "see, there's a happy ending, except for my abandonment issues."

"You: abandonment. Me: mnemophobia. We are just perfectly broken," she said playfully.

In the produce section she grabbed a couple of kiwis. Ryan wrinkled his nose which Dove immediately observed.

"What's wrong?" she asked.

"Oh nothing, just that kiwi has to be the worst fruit on earth. Eating a ball of fur is just not okay."

"No way... try bananas," Dove said, "The smell is just putrid."

They argued back and forth until each dared the other to try one without vomiting.

"And if I win?" Dove asked.

"Then I owe you dinner," Ryan smiled, "...and if I win, I get to kiss you after I take you to dinner," he added.

They stared at each other for an immeasurable moment of time, anticipation running through each of their minds.

"Deal," she agreed, forsaking her heart's warning that she was moving too fast.

Then like reckless teenagers, they began chomping on the fruit they despised, each trying to not to gag. Dove barely swallowed half and she tried hard to suppress her need to gag with each bite. They both erupted in laughter at how silly they were being but for the moment it seemed they had resolved their struggles with memories. One fighting to remember, the other fighting to forget.

She grabbed a few other things before making her way to the register.

"Bird!" the voice called from behind her.

"Aunt Dana," she smiled broadly.

Besides a few old classmates, Dana was the only other person she knew that consistently called her Bird.

Dana carefully looked the young man over. It was strange for her to see Dove with another man other than her son. She couldn't help but feel a bit of resentment towards the man. But much like the story that was sold to her friends, she had been told Dove suffered an injury that caused her loss of memory. It saddened her that Dove hadn't remembered her or Quilt, but she loved her and wouldn't want to hurt her, as she had been warned that forcing her memory could do more harm than good.

"Aunt Dana, this is Ryan... a friend."

He was pleased that he had been promoted from 'a neighbor'.

"Nice to meet you Ryan," she smiled lazily.

The two ladies spoke for a few minutes while Ryan paid for the items.

"Anything coming back on the memories?"

"Not yet," she replied sadly.

"Well, I love you Bird. You just remember that." She squeezed her tightly before she walked away towards the frozen food aisle.

* * *

They pulled into the driveway and Dove noticed that her car was gone. Ryan assured her again that her car was in good hands and helped her with the groceries and even helped her put things away.

She rinsed the strawberries and ate a few. She had forgotten that she missed breakfast and lunch. She offered to make him something to eat but he declined. He had promised to help his aunt with a task.

She really wanted him to stay. Dove enjoyed his company, but she understood his need to go. Dove walked him to the door and thanked him for taking her shopping.

"You're welcome," he turned to face her, and they locked eyes before his fingers drifted to her mouth.

His thumb wiped away a trace of strawberry from her lips. The air was so still that she could hear him breathe. His hand was steady as it slowly traced down the side of her neck. She could feel her heart trying to escape her chest. His hand found the nape of her neck, pulling her closer.

You're moving too fast! her heart screamed, but she was incapable of resisting. She was frozen.

His lips lingered on hers, tracing the outline with faint kisses before delving deeper, until they came up for air.

"I couldn't wait until dinner," he smiled.

She smiled back at him.

Like lemonade on a hot summer day... it was enough to quench his thirst. But he wanted more. For now, he would wait.

CHAPTER FOURTEEN

Those Stubborn Memories

It had been a week since Dove had seen Ryan. A week since he had left her breathless with a kiss. His uncle had taken a turn for the worst and they had gone on a trip to New York to see a specialist for his disease.

He was sure to text her every morning and night, except today.

She had hoped everything was okay, and on her way to meet Robyn for dinner she drove by the Westbrook's house, but the lights were still off. The car was still missing from the driveway.

During lunch, Robyn wasted very little time in grilling her about Ryan. Dove answered every one of her questions while checking her phone frequently. How could she miss someone so terribly that she had only known for such a short time?

It was the perfect spring day. They sat at the outside cafe where they could bask in the sunlight. The breeze blew tenderly, and lilac swept the air with a gentle fragrance from the nearby shrubs.

Dove checked her phone one last time before deciding to put it away. She would not let a missing text ruin her day, although it already had. She took a quick sip of her drink after the waiter placed it on the table. His eyes meeting hers more than once, in a way that could possibly be mistaken as flirting on her part. He smiled with every encounter.

"Excuse me but have met before?" she asked.

She hadn't paid much attention at the first greeting but now, her phone wasn't a distraction and she felt pretty sure she knew him.

"No, can't say we have," he said in a deep southern accent, "besides, I would never forget a pretty face." He smiled and there it was again, she thought. Familiarity!

She was sure they had met.

"I don't know, you look awfully familiar," she replied.

Robyn noticed it too. His naturally thick eyebrows that made them look magnetic, the way he tilted his head when he smiled. It was such an uncanny resemblance to Quilt.

"I wouldn't mind getting to know you more though," he said playfully.

Dove suddenly felt awkwardly shy, relinquishing the eye contact they was sharing. His boldness made her blush.

Robyn cleared her throat. "Chris, would you mind bringing me another glass of water."

"Sure," he said. He smiled at Dove before leaving the table.

"What is wrong with you? He's like nineteen at most," Robyn said.

"I wasn't the one flirting," Dove laughed.

She had no intention of dating a nineteen-year-old, but it sure made her feel desirable. Especially after not hearing from Ryan. She peeked at her phone in her bag and still there was no text.

"Are you taking your medicine?" Robyn asked. Fearing that her sister was starting to remember.

Dove assured her that her health was her number one priority.

The sisters nibbled on their salads, drank till they were full and topped it off with a free cheesecake they shared for dessert.

On the way out, Chris was at the table in front of them. Dove walked past him, taking a quick look back at his face. He winked at her, causing her to giggle to herself as she walked away. She had no doubt that in the boy's mind, she really desired him.

They finally left for home after she helped Robyn shop for art decor which seemed to take up most of the daylight hours. Shopping with Robyn was always a complicated task. She was very precise on whatever she wanted, and she didn't compromise, not even a little.

Though she was happy she had gotten out and spent the day with her older sister, her feet hurt, and she couldn't wait to get into bed.

After soaking in the bath for a while, Dove got dressed in her red tank top and flannel shorts to match. She massaged her feet then slid them in her favorite pair of fuzzy socks.

She vowed not to check her phone for the rest of the night, but that would change when a series of alerts was heard coming from her purse. Her face lit brighter than the sun on a ninety-eight-degree day.

Ryan: Hello star in the night sky.

Ryan: I've missed you today.

Dove: I've missed you too. Everything okay?

Ryan: Yes, have good news to share.

She was happy for him. She knew how much his uncle meant to him. Mr. Westbrook was his father's only relative that had volunteered to raise the siblings in order to keep them out of foster care.

The man meant the world to him.

Dove: I can't wait to see you, so you can share.

Ryan: I can't wait either. Would swim across oceans and climb mountains to see you right now and...

Her heart melted, and she sat for a moment smiling like a Cheshire cat, a smile that lingered forever until it was wiped away by the sound of the doorbell.

"...I did." Ryan said. He stood smiling on her doorstep. In his hand a bouquet filled with lilies. Somehow, he had found out they were her favorite.

And before she could speak, he had her in his arms, engulfing her entire body. There was hunger, hungry eyes, hungry lips. He pulled back for a minute and both were breathing heavily.

"I need you to let me in!"

She moved to the side of the door.

He smiled nervously.

"No, not like inside of your house," he fumbled, "I want you to let me in... inside of your heart. Tonight, I want long conversations. I want to know all your fears... what scares you the most, because I want to be the one to protect you. I want you to fall asleep on my chest. I want to watch you sleep and, in the morning, I want to be there. To be the first one you see when you open your eyes." His face was intense, "...and I know we've only known each other a short time and this... this memory loss still haunts you, but what I'm saying Dove is that I want us to make new ones."

She placed her hand on her heart, to quiet the flutters of the butterflies. "Come in," she looked him in his eyes and whispered. This time she would pull him through the door.

* * *

They met the following day and the two would meet again every day for the next six months.

Ryan planned a tripped to Seattle, meticulously planned it on a day that it wouldn't rain. He wanted her to see more than just cloudy skies. He took her to his favorite cafe where she tried the world's best coffee. They visited the Seattle Center where she danced along with the water show. He made her conquer her fears of height by taking her to the Space Needle Center. After showing her a glimpse of the world from five hundred and twenty feet, he took her to the restaurant just below the observation deck.

Dove gazed at Ryan, she found that he was less talkative than usual. The man had barely heard the questions she had asked him. He must have rubbed his forehead a hundred times. Puddles of sweat erupted and dripped from his face like a faulty facet. His skin was tinted with the shade of spring foliage hue. *Are you feeling sick?* She wanted to ask him again, but he quickly excused himself before she had the chance.

Ryan was standing over the bathroom sink, the porcelain supporting his tall frame. A small box resting on top. The sign that he wanted her to be his wife, something he had known from the moment he sat down beside her on their first date.

In his head, he practiced his speech for what seemed like the hundredth time... then doubt clouded his mind and oozed through his mouth like word vomit. "What if she says no? What if..."

There were two guys in the bathroom with him. "You won't know if you don't ask," said the man washing his hands at the sink next to him. His grey hair made him appear wise, the wedding band on his finger said he had experience.

Ryan looked at him and nodded. The other guy said a few encouraging words. They told him that it was the best thing in the world to find a soul mate. Ryan smiled, his insides erupting from the immeasurable amount of happiness that he had found.

Even though he didn't think of himself as marriage material, apparently, and to his immense surprise, he wanted her forever. The notion of bachelorhood had been abandoned. Now he saw himself as a husband, a protector, a father.

And when his fears subsided, he threw cold water on his face and muscled up enough courage to go ask the woman of his dreams to marry him. The guys offered to buy him a drink either way. They knew it was damn near impossible to predict a woman's answer.

Dove was sitting alone at the table. In between sipping on her Moscato and enjoy the view as the restaurant rotated, she wondered if Ryan was doing okay. He had been in the bathroom an awfully long time. She was one bad decision away from going into the men's bathroom and checking on him.

She was halfway out her chair when she noticed Ryan heading towards her. His brows were crouching over his brooding dark eyes and it seemed he had made some friends.

Before she could speak, he was kneeling before her, a gold box holding a diamond ring that glistened even without the light from the sun. She remembered hearing Ryan speak, and though she was sure the words were beautiful, she didn't hear much before the words *will you marry me?*

It felt as if more than the restaurant was spinning and she reminded herself to breathe. This was unexpected, but this was what she had hoped for, though not this soon. Yet, she was certain that Ryan was the one she wanted for eternity. Tears washed her face and she smiled broadly. Then she realized he was still waiting on her to answer and so was the group of glowering strangers.

"Yes!" she shouted, "yes... I'll be with you forever."

And the word forever was one of the words that he wanted to hear for the rest of his life.

There was the sound of applause, and he kissed the woman he had named his blue flame. She had become his oxygen, heat and light. She burned so deeply inside his soul that it ignited a fire that he never knew existed.

CHAPTER FIFTEEN

A Room Without Shade

It was two days before the big move and Dove found that she was more eager now than she had ever been. The move was a leap she would take with Ryan. Another city, an escape, a chance to build new memories without being haunted by the ones that had abandoned her. Not that she was banishing her old memories, at least what was left of them, but she had also grown very weary of hearing herself ask: "How do I know you again?"

So many times, it felt as if she was on the verge of a break through with recalling certain milestones: Her graduation, prom, college years. They all felt as if they were linked to something, maybe someone of importance. She tried desperately to hold onto the haunting shadows but it was like grasping at smoke... poof! And it all disappeared. A face would slowly appear from the darkness then step back as soon as it saw even a faint light. It was as if the shadow was somewhat afraid.

Maybe a woman... or a man. The shadow often betrayed her, so she decided she would lock them away in a box forever. Old memories had become the ashes of time. This brought her peace. Where there was the gigantic crater in her life, Ryan had filled all of it. She felt whole again.

She placed her house on the market and found a beautiful modern home in the Southside of Seattle. The couple had searched many homes but immediately fell in love with the three-bedroom home with the lovely extended windows. The massive front porch had only made her fall in love with it even more. She envisioned herself with Ryan, sitting outside on the porch swing until the skies were completely covered with stars.

She couldn't wait for this new life, though she was plagued with reservation of leaving her family.

Six p.m. and guests were starting to arrive for the farewell dinner. Dove specifically remembered begging her mother not to have a party. She would've much rather say some individual goodbyes, but now she was sure she would have an emotional breakdown in front of the twelve guests.

For the past week she had stayed in her old bedroom which had brought back so many memories from her teenage years. Not much had changed. The flowery drapes still lined the windows, the poster of her favorite band remained untouched on the walls, and the air still carried the scent of potpourri. On the bedside tables were new lamps. Of that she was certain. The blue lamp shade added a touch of tranquility to the old room.

She glanced at the picture of her dad and she smiled remembering the feeling of being safe that always came with his hugs. She wished he was there to share in her moment, though she knew in her heart he would've approved of Ryan.

"Raye, can I borrow your ruby earrings?"

"Top draw, left side," Raven replied while she focused on her reflection in the vanity mirror as she applied her make up. She turned around when she caught a glimpse of her sister in the mirror. "Don't you look ravishing," she purred. "That green dress really cinches you in the right places."

Dove giggled and kissed Raven's cheek. "Thanks Raye, I'll keep these safe," she assured her before hurrying through the door.

Raven was immensely happy to see her sister's glow. All the deception and lies now somehow seemed justified. She had come to see that her mother was right... it gave Dove a chance at living.

She slipped on her chiffon black dress, adjusting the straps as she did a slow twirl in the mirror. Then she noticed it... the bird peering through the pane. It was perched on her window sill, looking in, proudly boasting the fiery redness painted on its chest.

Slowly, Raven walked towards the window, hoping not to scare it away. Dove's words echoed inside her head. It was something about *Quilt visiting her in the form of a bird.*

She had dismissed her sister as being utterly crazy but couldn't help but think, *what if life really existed in another realm, and the darkest things like shadows and spirits weren't really meant to scare us?* She thought, and then she shuddered at the cold chill that ran along her arms.

Raven leant towards the window and with her hands upon her knees she leaned in closer.

"Quilt?" she whispered softly, "Matthew is that you?"

"Who is Mathew?" Dove asked entering the room to find her sister staring out the window.

Raven hesitated. She quickly gathered her thoughts. *Who is Matthew?* She repeated in her head.

"Oh... someone I went to school with. I just saw him going into the Peterson's house." She replied as she turned to face Dove.

"Okay, well Ryan is here, I'm heading down. Are you ready?" Dove asked nonchalantly as she fidgeted with the necklace in her hand.

"I'll be down in a few."

"See you in a few," Dove emphasized.

Raven returned to the window, but the bird had gone away. She began to laugh at the silly notion that she had somehow thought the bird was Quilt. She knew better; that Dove had suffered a mental breakdown during that time she had spoken that idea. But what was her excuse? She had none.

* * *

The table was set with gourmet meals which everyone began to devour. Besides forced conversation, questions from guests, and a teenager who was constantly trying to escape the table, dinner was going well.

The Westbrooks looked like they belonged. They made several delightful jokes at Ryan's expense. He seemed to enjoy the large group of family. He was happy. Dove could tell, and not because he had kissed her hand a thousand times, but there was a sparkle that never left his eyes.

She was happy too and besides the occasional cold stare that Aunt Dana threw her way, she really was enjoying having everyone around.

"Can someone pour me a fresh drink, this one has been sitting since the beginning?" Dana said but not loud enough to be heard over the multiple conversations.

She snatched the bottle of wine from the table and poured another drink.

"Fresh is better, right Dove?" she asked as she took a sip to swallow the bitter taste that was in her mouth.

Dove smiled weakly... her aunt was making her uncomfortable although she didn't know why.

Dana, on the other hand, knew exactly why. She was filled with resentment. Her daughter-in-law had moved on and though she didn't blame Dove for her memory loss, she had felt alone trying to keep her son's memory alive, and she was forced to not even mention his name. He had been forgotten. Keeping his memory alive was something she had hoped her and Dove would always share. Now her son was being replaced with someone new and she didn't care for him much.

"Oh, that ring!" she exclaimed as she looked at Dove's hand. She held her hand as she examined the diamond. "Certainly not like paper," her smile was sinister.

Dove politely pulled her hand away, then she reached for her glass to take a sip.

"That's beautiful Bird... guess some birds are meant to be caged," she winked.

The glass slipped from between Dove's trembling fingers. Her punch coating the cloth like paint splattered on a wall.

The room fell silent.

The teenager finally found her reason to escape.

Dove's head was pounding as if someone had just kicked in the barricade and now her head was flooded... but with pain... with memories. It filled her lungs. She gasped to breathe, and she swallowed the liquid in her throat.

The shadow, a man, showed her quick flashes of things: Her prom, paper rings, origami, lanterns on a beach, wedding bands... and then he showed her Ryan's face, smiling, kissing her hand. His voice was silvery as he repeated the exact words of Dana.

She still couldn't see his face. *Who are you?* She pleaded with him. *What's your name? Why won't you show me your face?*

Dove massaged the scar at the back of her head. The pain had become excruciating. The flood now poured through her eyes and she ran to her room to escape the worried faces.

Ryan chased after her. He caught her hand at the stairs and he begged her to let him help.

"I just need a few minutes alone," she told him.

At the table, Ryan glowered angrily at Dana. He wasn't quite sure what she had done but something she did had triggered Dove's reaction and he felt sure of it.

"What the hell did you say to her?" he yelled, and it felt like the entire house shook.

Mr. Westbrook tried to calm his nephew down and an anxious Mrs. Williams ushered Dana to her office. Moments later, an emotional Dana emerged from the room and went straight for the door. Mrs. Williams followed soon after and she thanked everyone for coming out.

* * *

Ryan checked on Dove a few times, but she had locked herself in her room assuring him each time that she would only be a few more minutes.

The guests had finally cleared, and he apologized to her family for the outburst.

Raven sat silently. Her stomach was tangled in knots. "I think it's time we told the truth?" she directed her question at Mrs.

Williams. Her voice sounded defeated. The kind of voice where you just feel like you want it all to end.

"Tell the truth about what?" Ryan asked, his forehead deeply creased.

"There's nothing to tell!" she scolded her daughter.

"Ryan!" Raven yelled in frustration as she leapt to her feet. "Dove was once married to a wonderful man. They were high school... no elementary school sweethearts. Well, she lost him over a year ago... it was a horrible accident and Dove just couldn't handle it. She sunk so far into her depression that she tried to take her life." Raven cried. "We just couldn't take losing her and what we did was inexcusable," she rubbed her burning chest.

Raven sat down and sighed. She felt a small sense of relief, though she knew sharing the rest with Dove would not be so easy.

"What did you do?" Ryan asked, and the room was ghostly silent.

"We suppressed her memory, every memory she had of him. It was no accident, it was us," Robyn revealed.

"This can't be real." He shook his head in disbelief, a hint of disgust in his voice. His head felt full as every ounce of blood rushed to his face, causing a vein to protrude on his forehead. His insides were on fire, a fire that he wasn't even capable of putting out. Ryan nostrils flared before he lashed out like a raging bull. And when he was done, his rage had been replaced by fear. The realization that the woman of his dreams had once loved so deep that she was willing to sacrifice her life to be with him.

This could change everything. If she remembers, would it change the way she felt about him?

Ryan suddenly felt weak. His back hit the back of the wall and he sunk until he was sitting on the hard floor.

"Ryan, I'm so sorry," Robyn said, and she moved closer to touch him.

He grunted at her to stay away.

He couldn't understand how a mother could've done this to a child, at least his ran away before she could do any harm. This situation just seemed highly cruel. His heart ached for his love and he knew she needed to know the truth, even if it meant that he would lose her.

It was the honorable thing to do.

* * *

Dove emerged from her room. Her eyes were now dry although tears stained her cheeks.

"I'm sorry," she apologized before hugging her fiancée. "I remembered something, and it scared me, but I won't let it scare me anymore." She turned towards her mother, her sisters avoided making eye contact. Inside they were ashamed but more frightened. "Have I ever been married?" she asked.

Mrs. Williams nodded. "Yes," she paused, "...and there's more."

Ryan hugged her from behind, wrapping her tightly in his arms as if he was somehow protecting her from a storm that was coming.

"Why don't I remember him?" Dove closed her eyes as if she was trying to retrieve the details from her past.

"Your memories of Quilt were causing you debilitating psychological problems. So much that you tried to end your life." Mrs. Williams explained. "After the second attempt, I just couldn't wait on a third." She sighed deeply before continuing "The medication that you have been taking to control your anxiety also works to suppress stress-related memories. It was supposed to be a temporary solution."

"Ryan..." she whispered as she stepped back to stay beyond her mother's reach.

"Dove," her mother cried upon noticing the tightness around Dove's eyes. "If you stop taking the medicine...." She paused as Dove waved a hand in dismissal.

"Robyn...Raye, did you know about this?" Dove asked

They both nodded and their eyes drifted to the floor to avoid the icy glare coming from Dove's eyes.

This was the most devasting loss Dove could remember. It was a purposeful act of betrayal. One that she did not want to forgive. The house fell silent and every sound coming from the outside was magnified as Dove pondered over the pieces the shadow had showed her.

She no longer desired to remember. It was if the man did not want to be found either... he wanted her to be happy.

Origami and paper rings would become ashes of things she had decided to burn. She knew for her to open a door, it first had to be closed. The shadow revealed that much. For the second time, Dove had buried her husband. Only this time she had placed him deeper than before.

"I was incredibly selfish to cause you all such pain, but it will take some time for me to get over this betrayal." she said to her family. "I will take some comfort in believing that maybe my deceased husband wasn't a kind person and maybe he deserved to be erased."

Raven eyes were fixated on her sister. Her mouth slightly open as if she wanted to speak but instead she nodded as she thought about things the old Dove would've have done. Old Dove would've snatched dishes from the table and broke more than just a few. She would've told Robyn where to shove her apology and she would've told her mother that she would never forgive her while spitefully burning rubber on her mother's precious lawn as she stormed away in her car. Raven missed the old Dove, though she had come to appreciate the fact that the new Dove was alive.

"I'm choosing to leave the memories in the past. My future is with Ryan."

"You're okay with this?" Ryan asked. Inside he was bursting with happiness. It felt as if she had chosen him and though he knew he was being selfish, he had secretly prayed that her memories would stay buried.

"Yes!" she beamed, "I want you forever."

In one sentence Dove had unknowingly eradicated his fear of abandonment.

"...and you're not angry?" he questioned through furrowed brows.

Dove was certainly angry, but something had changed. Something that made the past seem almost unimportant. Dove had discovered that she was pregnant.

"I am most certainly angry but I have you," she laughed giddily as she stroked both sides of his face.

"Yes, you do." He agreed, and he cupped her face, kissing her lips. He didn't care that he was confused about her reaction. His insides were bursting with joy. He would get to marry his one true love.

"Ryan," she said, "I'm pregnant."

A smile as big as the ocean surfed a crossed his face. Euphoria taking complete control.

"Are you sure?" he stuttered "when?"

"Just now, in my room. I took the test."

He lifted her high in the air; spinning her around before showering her with hugs.

Mrs. Williams observed her daughter. This was the outcome she had hoped for; this kind of happiness is what her Dove deserved. She wanted to hold her daughter but she knew Dove still needed time.

CHAPTER SIXTEEN

Cardinal Signs

Ryan paced back and forth at the altar. His legs were shaking with each step he took. He tucked his hands in his pockets to hide the jitteriness.

Malcolm, his best man, did everything to keep him calm. He had been there before, and of course he wanted to tease his friend for being so nervous, but he himself had been there before and it was simple; he understood. A sympathetic grin slowly crossed his face as he watched as his best friend paced back and forth. "Any minute now," he assured Ryan while running his thumb over small the velvet box.

Ryan smile was weak. The wait was killing him. "A minute is starting to feel like forever... I might pass out." He knew he was being watched... eyes were everywhere, and he nervously waved to the group of onlookers.

He wondered how many of them had seen a grown man cry.

He tilted his head towards the ceiling, closed his eyes and took a deep breath to calm his anxiety. And when he opened them...

she was strolling down the aisle of the First Baptist Church on top of a runner that lit up with each step.

She was the most beautiful woman he had ever laid eyes on.

Ryan thought about the wedding movies he had seen, and about the few real-life weddings he had attended, but never had he imagined that he could be so completely awestruck.

Up until this moment he had been sure he had been in love before... but feeling this cascade of joy that flowed within him made him question the authenticity of those previous feelings. She was undoubtedly, his grace.

He tried to fight the tears, but they were stronger and now he knew, with absolute certainty that now one hundred and eighty people had seen a grown man cry.

"Those better be tears of joy," Dove teased as she took her place next to her groom.

He nodded... words had failed him.

Her Uncle lifted her white veil and for a moment the light hit her eyes from the stained-glass window and she saw her father's face, that he had once lifted her veil before.

Uncle Paul kissed her cheek and placed her safely in the hands of Ryan.

"You are perfect," Ryan whispered.

For the rest of the ceremony she was the only person he saw. Dove was the only thought that flowed through his mind. The nine-year-old boy inside of him celebrated as they exchanged vows. He had found his bond.

* * *

The guess arrived at the outdoor reception, each wearing the pin of a blue flame. They all dazzled in white as the couple had requested to celebrate rebirth.

Coastal clouds rolled across the wondrous sky. The tinge of orange began to fade with the disappearing sun. Dainty paper lights added a surplus of colors to the pathway to the dance floor.

Birds were singing, and the heavens opened, but all were lost to the chattering of the party as the crowds were buzzing about how beautiful the bride had looked and the wonderful ceremony. A sweet rendition of forever mine could be heard from the violinist under the gazebo.

Raven weaved through the crowd, holding onto the two filled glasses of champagne in her hand. She handed one to Kevin who had seemed preoccupied by something in the tree.

"Now that something to defy science."

"What?" she asked out of curiosity.

"A Northern cardinal... and they say that the bird doesn't migrate," he said, taking the glass from her hand.

Raven looked towards the tree to see the bird with its flaming red chest. She followed its gaze towards the married couple amid their first dance. And she watched for minutes before it flew away towards the wide-open sky.

Raven rested her head on her boyfriend's chest, spilling champagne as they swayed. Her gaze fixated on the heavens above.

"Kevin. Do you believe in reincarnation?" she asked.

"I believe in many possibilities my love. Why?" he asked.

She wanted to tell him of the story she had created in her mind... that Quilt had somehow returned as a bird, to somehow fulfill his promise to Dove. To give her everything he could to make her happy. He brought her Ryan, a baby she had longed for, this wedding and now... he was gone.

And even if it was pure fantasy, it felt right in her mind, because it was exactly the man Quilt was.

She smiled at the clouds as they parted and waved goodbye with their invisible hands. Then she became overwhelmed with gratitude that her sister had forgiven her.

* * *

'Winter charged in like the bull upon the matador.

She was clothed in dark attire – her cloak, the darkest of grey with thickness to shield her from the light of the sun.

In her hand she bore a large piece of solidified water. The tip was sharp and spiked.

Then....in one quick swipe; she silenced autumn.

She was cold!

After all, she had a reputation to uphold.

Winter froze hearts and painted many things blue.

She wasn't likeable. In her eyes everyone loved summer.

But summer needed to rejuvenate. She needs her beautiful rest.

And though the two had never met. What she knew for sure was that summer was loud and obnoxious. And most of all she was filth.

So, she vowed to rid the Earth of her musty stench.

Autumn, she knew, and she was much too weak and... Spring whom she had met, was far too kind. Always prancing around like some giddy headed child.

Winter sent rain and she made it pour and then she dusted the land with snow.

From morning until night... It snowed.

Then morning came.'

Dove paused for a minute. It sounded as if Ryan had called her name. She placed a book mark between her pages and headed towards the next room.

An exuberant Ryan was moving to music as he swiped the paint brush back and forth. His shirtless back was stained with yellow paint and she stood admiring him for a moment. He kept painting, oblivious to her presence in the room. She stepped closer, the heavy rain masking the sound of her footsteps. She hugged him from behind, then removed the earphones that were tucked securely in his ears. Her large stomach bore into his back.

"Looks like someone is happy to see me," he teased.

She giggled heartily. She adored how he made her laugh.

Ryan placed the paint brush in the pan and he led her away from the paint fumes.

His eyes met hers with concern. "Everything okay?" he asked.

"Yes, just thought I heard you call my name."

He smiled "Nope," he replied, "I think you just really miss me." he stroked the tip of her nose.

"Did you finish your book?"

"No, my back is starting to act up again."

"Why don't I run you a nice warm bath?"

She was three days away from her due date. Her anxiety level had skyrocketed the last couple of days. The stories and videos about the pain of childbirth had only made matters worse.

He helped her into the bathtub and watched her sink into the comfort of the warm water. He rubbed her stomach as delightful little feet moved around with excitement.

"Are you scared?" he asked.

"Terrified!" she sighed.

"I am too." He grabbed the sponge, massaging her back with each stroke.

"If I could trade places with you, I would, just so you wouldn't feel any pain," he told her, "but I can't, so I, Ryan Westbrook give you, Dove Westbrook, permission to kick, punch and curse at me."

"I'm loving all three options," she said, and both laughed.

His tone got serious. "You're an amazing woman Dove, and I really don't deserve you."

"You really don't," she teased, and he laughed gloriously. The kind of laughter that only existed in someone who had an overabundance of happiness.

He helped her finish her bath before tucking her in bed. He handed her the book she had been trying so hard to finish.

'Then morning came...

Winter was in for a surprise.

She witnessed little boys throwing snowballs, a toddler, desperately trying to catch the snow on his tongue and he squealed with delight when he finally made success.

A father was building a snowman, and little girls all dolled up in their festive layered clothing were dancing in the snow.

Winter's heart began to melt at the realization that she too was loved.

And she pledged that she would give retribution for all the things she had broken.

So, she released her anger and allowed spring to come in.

Rebirth! Redemption! Reincarnation.

She closed the book, feeling a sense of accomplishment that she finally finished. Yet something resonated about the story so loud that she herself felt that things that had been stripped away had now been redeemed. It had been months since she stopped taking the medications, yet her old memories had remained buried.

She made her way out the bathtub to find Ryan had laid out her nightgown, and a cup of fresh steaming tea had been placed on the night stand. Next to it lay a note that simply read: I love you.

It was enough to settle her fears. She sank underneath the comfort of her covers where she quickly fell asleep.

CHAPTER SEVENTEEN

Revelation

The feel of something squeezing her stomach was enough to wake Dove out of her sleep, but as quickly as it came it disappeared. She rolled over to eye the clock. It was six in the morning and she barely felt as if she had got enough sleep.

"Ryan," she mumbled drowsily.

Her snoring husband seemed to be in deep sleep, his body stretching all over the bed with bare legs that hung over the edge.

Another sharp pain moved like a wave across her abdomen, this time radiating to her back and it forced her to change her position. She stood up and slowly made her way towards the bathroom.

And that's when it happened... a gush of liquid trickled down her leg.

"Ryan," she yelled. Her eyes were now open wide as if she was transformed into a frightened child.

Ryan mumbled some undetectable words, but his eyes remained closed.

She moved closer to the bathroom but a wave, no, a titanic, seized her and bought her to her knees. It felt as if someone was ripping her insides with just bare hands.

"Ryan," she screamed louder, for what seemed like eternity.

He slowly opened his eyes. A part of him felt like he was dreaming until he heard his wife's continuous heavy breathing. He was still a little dazed and confused as he jumped out of the bed.

He darted over to where she was curled up like a ball on the carpet. His heart beat unevenly… like a galloping horse.

"Dove!" he cried.

"I... think... it's... time," she said through uneven breaths.

He was blank. All the things they had prepared for this day suddenly escaped him.

"Ryan… call Dr. Martin," she said calmly.

"Yes, call Dr. Martin," he said with confirmation, and he rushed to retrieve the phone from the nightstand. His fingers trembled. His brain was clearly out of sync with the rest of his body and he struggled to find the doctor's number.

"How far apart are the contractions?" he asked.

"About every fifteen minutes!" Dove shouted gritting her teeth as she struggled to breathe through another event that paralyzed her lower half.

Ryan carefully repeated the timing back to the physician. He couldn't help to feel responsible for creating this tiny human who seemed to be ripping his wife's insides apart, but he couldn't wait to meet his little one.

He lifted Dove to the bed. "She wants us to come in when you are closer to five minutes," he said, reminding himself to sound calm although inside he was terrified, on the outside he now appeared composed. He had to be strong for her.

He threw on some of her favorite songs. Ryan helped her shower, twisted her hair as he gave her a single braid and reminded her to breathe through the pain as they dreadfully await on the contractions to come closer and faster than a speeding train. When it was time, Ryan had gotten his mind and strength in coordination as he carefully got through the door.

Dove had grown weary. It was now after six p.m. and she was still at six centimeters. She couldn't recall a time that she had been more exhausted, even being unsure if she still possessed the capability to push. They had checked her cervix a dozen times, but she was still not fully dilated.

Ryan sat silently, allowing his wife to crush his fingers with each contraction, he wanted to scream for bloody mercy. She wasn't the only one feeling the pains of labor, although he dared not say it out loud.

"Good news," he said as she laid quietly fighting sleep. "Your family was able to book a late flight for tonight. They'll be here in the morning."

Her eyes were closed. He released the grip on his hand and wiped away the beads of sweat on her forehead. She looked so peaceful and he could not have adored her more than he did in that moment.

A few minutes later the doctor entered the room, awakening his wife from her three-minute nap.

Dr. Martin checked her cervix again and this time a bright beam crossed her face.

"We're at ten!" she exclaimed.

Ryan was even more nervous than he had been, excitement filled him inside. He was getting ready to meet his child they had decided that boy or girl wouldn't matter, they had just prayed for a healthy baby.

The moon reared its head in the sky, peeking inside of the oval window. A zillion star lined the sky, shining excitedly, as if they waited to accept this birth into the universe.

Dove pushed and screamed, and when she thought she could, she breathed so much that she started hyperventilating, but Ryan's soothing words would provide some comfort, about as much comfort that one can expect from a mother being torn apart inside.

Push... breathe... push! She repeated the sequence until she heard the most beautiful cries that had been laid upon her ears.

He was covered in specks of blood and white goo, but he was the most beautiful baby boy she had ever seen. And when they placed him on her chest, her flaccid arms mustered up enough strength to comfort the tiny human she had brought into the world. And when she inhaled every bit of her child, he was scooped from her arms by one of the nurses.

Through barely open eyes she watched as they measured his footprints. She fell in love instantly with his tiny little toes. She looked up at the proud look on Ryan's face when they placed his son in his arms. Then exhaustion gave in and she was off to replenish, finding the sleep that her body so desperately needed.

* * *

"Hi Darling," the voice whispered as she blinked a few times trying to open her lids. She was still so drowsy from some degree of exhaustion. She wiped her eyes to clear the fuzzy view.

Mrs. Williams smiled at her while her sisters were making kissy faces with their new nephew and baby talking as a gloating Ryan held the baby proudly in his arms.

"Hey Mom."

"You've been sleeping for a while now, even missed breakfast."

She looked at the clock: Eleven; Eleven.

"I guess I was exhausted." She sat upward in the bed.

"There's mommy," Ryan smiled at the baby as he brought him closer to her.

He kissed his wife and placed the baby in her arms. The two had only seen each other briefly since last night.

"What a beautiful baby boy," she said. Something was so familiar. It was as if she had known him all her life... had seen his eyes before.

Besides Ryan's lips... she couldn't tell whose eyes they were. They were round and brown.

The boy struggled to stare in his mother's face. She could not stop admiring his eyes, so innocent as if you could see all the way to his soul. Maybe they were his grandfather's eyes. But no, she thought, *Daddy had wide set eyes.*

A single tear rolled down her cheek. Memories hit her hard, like walking into a brick wall.

It was everything at once... everything flooded the sea of memories, not at all in small doses.

"Quilt," she said out loud.

"Bird," the shadow in her head answered back to her as he stepped out into the light.

Now it all made sense. A thousand origami flooded her mind along with the cardinal bird that had been a constant presence in her life. Quilt was her soulmate and he represented everything that was good.

"Thank you." She whispered. Dove closed her eyes as she remembered climbing on a sturdy chair that somehow had break and prevented the rope from tightening around her neck.

He smiled broadly as his presence blended into the light. "I love you Bird."

"Goodbye Quilt. Rest peacefully my love."

She gripped Ryan's hand tightly, pulling him towards her. It was forceful but she didn't care. Dove wanted him to know that she remembered everything and of the overwhelming happiness she felt for the match made in heaven.

www.ingramcontent.com/pod-product-compliance
Lightning Source LLC
Chambersburg PA
CBHW020941310726
48980CB00001B/9

* 9 7 8 0 5 7 8 5 1 4 3 8 3 *